'What did you expect, Melly? That I would forgive and forget?'

'Tell you that I didn't mind being used? Well, I do mind,' Charles gritted almost savagely. 'I mind like hell! I liked you! Trusted you! And now I find I can't even bear to be near you without wanting to smash something! As soon as the baby's born, we'll go our separate ways. I don't think I ever want to see you again!'

Dear Reader

In this year of European unity, July sees the launch in hardback (September paperback) of an intriguing new series—contemporary romances by your favourite Mills & Boon authors, but with a distinctly European flavour. Look out for the special cover of a love story every month set in one of the twelve EC countries, which will take you on a fascinating journey to see the sights, life and romance, Continental style.

Vive l'amour in 1992—who do *you* think is Europe's sexiest hero?

The Editor

Emma Richmond was born during the war in north Kent when, she says, 'Farms were the norm and motorways non-existent. My childhood was one of warmth and adventure. Amiable and disorganised, I'm married with three daughters, all of whom have fled the nest— probably out of exasperation! The dog stayed, reluctantly. I'm an avid reader, a compulsive writer and a besotted new granny. I love life and my world of dreams, and all I need to make things complete is a housekeeper— like, yesterday!'

MORE THAN
A DREAM

BY

EMMA RICHMOND

MILLS & BOON LIMITED
ETON HOUSE   18-24 PARADISE ROAD
RICHMOND   SURREY   TW9 1SR

*First published in Great Britain 1992
by Mills & Boon Limited*

© Emma Richmond 1992

*Australian copyright 1992
Philippine copyright 1992
This edition 1992*

ISBN 0 263 77646 8

*Set in Times Roman 11 on 12 pt.
01-9208-49851 C*

Made and printed in Great Britain

CHAPTER ONE

'ALL right?'

'Yes, I'm fine, truly.'

'Sure you don't want to come?'

'Sure,' Melly confirmed with a smile. 'Go on, you go; have a good time.'

'We-ell, all right, if you're sure.'

'I am. Go.'

With an answering smile, he kissed her quickly on the mouth, grabbed his car keys, and left.

So punctilious, so polite, so eager to be away. With no one now to see, the shadows returned to her lovely amber eyes. Getting to her feet, she walked across to the window in order to watch his slim, elegant figure stride from the house; to note the casual way he pushed back his dark hair before climbing behind the wheel of his beloved XJS, and continue to watch as he roared off down the drive. Charles. Her husband. The man she adored to the point of insanity. The man who did not love her. Did he have any idea at all, she wondered, what his kisses did to her? How she stored them up like a miser? No, she doubted he ever gave them a thought. With a rather wry, sad little smile, she smoothed her palm gently over the burgeoning swell of her stomach.

Charles, whom she had comforted on the death of his closest friend in a yachting accident. Charles, who had made love to her in his anguish and pain, and then married her when he'd discovered she was pregnant. Charles, whom she had loved since the age of ten, but who would never have considered marrying her had it not been for the baby.

With a long sigh, she drew the heavy brocade curtains across the window before returning to the large leather armchair drawn up before the fire. Sitting awkwardly, she tucked her legs beneath her. Charles's chair, which she had, to his amusement, adopted as her own. Her eyes on the dried flowers in the empty fireplace, she saw only Charles. Visualised him parking outside the casino, striding in, grinning at his friends and acquaintances. Relaxed, casual, elegant. Adored. A man liked by women; envied by men. A man who had probably forgotten all about her, she thought with another little smile. A care-for-nobody... No, that wasn't true, that was just the impression he liked to give, a mask he showed the world. Why, she did not know, only that it was true. Because he thought nobody cared for him? Perhaps, but what she did know was that there was a great deal more to Charles than met the eye. Or was she interpreting facts to suit herself? Because she wanted to believe he was something he wasn't? Because he was attractive, with a wicked charm, and because she had always liked him, had she made him the misunderstood hero? Assumed his parents were tyrants because they had disowned him? Yet wasn't it likely that his parents had known him better than anyone? And, working on that assumption, wasn't it possible that it was not Charles who had been misunderstood, but his parents? Recalling to mind their prim mouths, their moralistic outlook, she shook her head. No, she would trust in Charles. And don't we all believe what we want to believe? she mocked herself. You no less than anyone else? Yet, even with the doubts, would she have changed anything that had happened these last few months? No. He would probably never love her as she longed to be loved, but he liked her, and, working on the principle that a few slices were better than no bread, she was probably as content as she would ever be.

He would care for her, and the child when it was born, but would he ever again share her bed? Ever again hold her close in his arms, when, even in his pain over the loss of his friend, he had proved himself a lover to surpass all others? She did not know, but she had made her bed, and now must lie on it.

Reaching out her hand, she tugged the little bell pull. It never failed to amuse her, the pretentiousness of it. Châtelaine. Of what? A small house that had no need of a butler, but had one all the same? Not, perhaps, in the image usually called to mind, but certainly quiet, mostly unobtrusive, and always elegantly attired. It was not a role, she often thought, that came naturally to him.

Entering quietly, he gave a small bow. '*Bonsoir, madame,*' he said with marvellous dignity, which was slightly spoilt by the hint of humour in his dark eyes.

'*Bonsoir, Jean-Marc.*' They had seen each other not fifteen minutes previously, and yet they always went through the same ritual. The same polite exchange. He was in his late fifties, she knew, but behaved as though he were seventy at least and a family retainer of long standing. He was slightly stocky, a little shorter than Charles, very French-looking, with dark hair and pale skin. He tried to give the very misleading impression of being aloof, and of never being hurried. Melly doubted either was true.

Charles had won him, along with the house, in a poker game, or so he said. Melly wasn't sure she believed him.

'*Je suis fatigué, Jean-Marc . . .*'

'*Madame* wishes to retire?'

'Jean-Marc! How am I ever going to learn to speak French properly if everyone persists in practising their English on me?'

With that wonderful Gallic shrug that was so difficult to imitate, and a downturning of his mobile mouth, he spread his hands in helpless enquiry.

With an infectious little chuckle, she nodded. 'Yes, I wish to retire.' Uncoiling herself, she stood and stretched. Of medium height, her once slim, almost boyish figure now nicely rounded, she lowered her arms and gave her gentle smile. Pushing the long brown curly hair away from her face, she asked hopefully, 'Hot milk?'

'Hot milk,' he confirmed with a look of disgust for her choice of beverage. 'I will bring it up to *madame* in—fifteen minutes?'

'Fifteen minutes will be fine. Goodnight, Jean-Marc.'

'*Bonsoir, madame.*'

Shaking her head at him, she went up to her room.

The milk was duly brought, and duly drunk. With a last smile for Jean-Marc as he left with the tray holding her empty glass, she settled herself in the large bed. But not to sleep. Or not until she heard Charles come in.

When she heard his quiet footstep on the stairs at just gone two she turned over and slept, which was why, when she woke in the morning, she still felt tired. She could, of course, have gone back to sleep. She didn't choose to. She always made a point of breakfasting with her husband. Even though he rarely returned from the casino, where he was one of the partners, before three, he was always up by eight o'clock, and now, after three months of marriage, it had become the norm for them to sit down together.

When she entered the dining-room he looked up from his seat at the table, and smiled. He looked delighted to see her. He looked delighted to see everyone. No comfort there.

With a lithe movement he got to his feet, walked to the opposite side of the table and held out her chair. As she sat he dropped a light kiss on the top of her head. 'Good morning, Melissa.'

'*Bonjour, Charles.*'

With a chuckle, he resumed his seat. 'Coffee?'

'Please.'

As with Jean-Marc, it was a ritual to be gone through. He poured the hot milk into her cup, with just a dash of coffee. Fresh warm croissants were piled in a snowy napkin in a basket in the centre of the table. There was butter, a selection of *confitures*, marmalade and honey. Charles reached for her plate, selected a croissant for her and placed it together with butter and honey in front of her. '*Bon appétit.*'

'*Merci.* You had a successful evening?'

'Mm, so-so. Not many in last night.'

'You played?'

'No, I wasn't feeling lucky. I mingled, talked to some people, listened to gossip,' and, for a moment, his generous mouth firmed. Not tightened; Charles's expressions were never excessive. He generally appeared relaxed, smiling, contented. It wasn't true that he was, of course—no one was ever that amiable—but if he had any dark thoughts, emotions, he hid them very well. Which was no doubt why he was such a good poker player. 'I've decided to move the horses to another *haras*.'

'But why?' she asked, puzzled. 'I thought you were quite happy with the way they were being trained. Heaven knows, you fought hard enough to get them into that particular stable!'

'Ye-es, but oh, I don't know, I have a feeling all is not well.'

Knowing better than to mock his 'feelings', she asked instead, 'Where will you place them?'

'Don't know; I'll have to give it more thought.' With the swift change of subject that was so characteristic of him, he smiled. 'I also saw Fabienne; she's invited us to dine tonight. Yes? I accepted for us both. You don't get out enough—and don't turn down your mouth, my darling, it's time you got over this reluctance you have to meet people.'

'I'm not reluctant to meet people, just...'

'Just those people who constitute my friends.'

'No,' she denied with a frown, 'that's not true; it's just that some of them...'

'Like Fabienne...'

'Yes, like Fabienne, make me feel—oh, I don't know, gauche, unsophisticated. I never know what to say to them.' Looking up, holding his grey eyes with her own, she added, 'You'll be much happier on your own.'

'Will I?' he asked with a quizzical smile.

'Yes. You won't need to worry about me, make sure I have someone to talk to, understand what's being said...' With a little smile and a shrug that was nowhere near as eloquent as Jean-Marc's, she left her sentence unfinished. But it was true: without her, he would thoroughly enjoy himself. Very gregarious was Charles. He liked meeting people, talking, exchanging ideas, and, although he had never by look or deed intimated that she was a drag on his enjoyment, she suspected he felt restricted by her presence. She had tried to overcome her not dislike, exactly, but discomfort with his smart friends, but she always got the feeling that they were sneering at her. Maybe she was being over-sensitive because of the circumstances of their marriage, but she could never feel quite at ease at these little dinner parties that everyone seemed to give.

'Nevertheless,' he said with a subtly different smile that meant he would expect her to go along with his wishes, 'I would like you to come. David will be there. You like David.'

Yes, she liked David; it was his wife she couldn't stand, mostly, she admitted, because the wretched Fabienne would persist in drooling all over Charles at every given opportunity. Touching, smiling, stroking, pressing herself against him as though she were irresistible, which she wasn't, not by any means. She was forty if she was a day and persisted in behaving as though she were sixteen. She seemed to be the violent exception to the rule that French woman were elegant, chic, sexy. Most older women that she had met were far more attractive than the younger set, having achieved that certain confidence and sophistication that wisdom brought, but not the wretched Fabienne, and, for all his perspicacity, Charles didn't seem to see what other women saw. That she was a troublemaker.

If Melly flatly refused he would still go, and he would say nothing more about it, but the smile would be cooler, the warmth that she needed withdrawn. She didn't think he knew that he did it, and maybe someone who did not know him very well would not notice. But she would. Forcing herself to smile, she nodded. 'All right, I'll come. What time?'

'Eightish. Thank you. I know it is not easy for you, Melly, but if you do not ever try you will not know...'

'What I'm missing,' she finished for him. 'I know, and I am trying; it's just that it's such a different lifestyle to the one I've been used to.'

'British understatement at its best,' he laughed. 'Beckford was hardly the Mecca of sophistication.' Leaning back in his chair, he steepled his fingers under his chin, a smile playing about his mouth. 'I would dearly love to know what they made of our marriage,' he mused.

'Oh, probably that I deserved all I got,' she said lightly. 'I mean, what else could one expect, marrying an adventurer?'

'Is that what they call me? An adventurer?'

'Mm.' A no-good adventurer, but she wasn't about to tell him that. Besides, it wasn't true.

With every appearance of enjoying the notoriety, he leaned forward and propped his chin in his hand. 'What else? Black sheep? Rogue? I bet they said, "Ah, that one, he'll come to no good. Meet a sticky end one day." Mm, I see by your face that I'm right. Well, it's possible I will one day fulfil their prophecies, but hopefully not drag you down with me. You deserve better, Melly.'

'No!' she said more sharply than she had intended. 'No,' she repeated more moderately.

'Yes,' he contradicted. 'If you had not come to Deauville to find your grandfather's grave; if——'

'If wishes were horses, beggars would ride,' she cut in firmly, because they both knew that *wasn't* why she had come. Charles might, for the sake of harmony, pretend to believe it, but she had always thought that he suspected otherwise. Always suspected that he was treading carefully, as she was, in order to make the marriage work. Holding his eyes, she forced herself to smile. 'You didn't coerce me. I didn't have to—comfort you that day. And if I had denied your paternity...'

'Ah, but you didn't, God knows why. Anyone less worthy to be a father would be hard to find. Anyone less worthy to be a husband... And yet, if you hadn't admitted it, if I had found out later that you were carrying my child...'

He would have been angry? Yes, she knew he would have been, and was sometimes very surprised by how responsible he seemed to feel. She desperately wished they could have spoken about it, discussed it, but because of her own feelings of guilt it always seemed impossible. And yet perhaps, after all, it was safer not to.

'How would you have found out?' she queried with a lightness she did not feel. 'You no longer had ties with Beckford, and as far as you knew I could have had any number of boyfriends, any one of whom could have been the father...'

'Maybe; water under the bridge now...' With an odd laugh, he straightened. 'Not exactly your normal run-of-the-mill husband, am I?'

'No,' she agreed with a forced smile, 'but then, run-of-the-mill might be a bit boring, don't you think?'

'And wouldn't you, if you were honest, not wish for boring now and again?' he asked whimsically. 'Like knowing where I was at nights? Or even days, come to that...?'

'But then you would never have won this house at poker; I would never have met Jean-Marc. Would never have ogled the rich and famous at the American Film Festival...'

'Ah, now, be fair, you could have ogled them any time. They hold the festival here every year.'

'But I couldn't have ogled them as a guest!' she insisted. 'Couldn't have ogled them from the arm of the most sought-after bachelor around. Anyway, I quite like being the wife of racehorse owner; the wife of a casino partner, famous yachtsman...'

'Hardly famous,' he derided, his mouth turned down at the corners.

'Well known, then,' she substituted. Staring at him, examining that strong, attractive face as he gazed pensively at the table, she wondered how much he was regretting it. Had he taken one too

many gambles and lost? Had he been expecting her
to refuse his proposal? He would never say, even
if she asked, yet she knew this wasn't the lifestyle
he had planned for himself. He'd been quite honest
about it, about never intending to marry. So really
he was someone else who had to lie in a bed of their
own making. 'You lost more than I ever could,' she
added quietly in a foolish desire to be reassured.
'Your freedom to choose.'

Raising his eyes, and shaking off whatever
thoughts he had been thinking, he smiled. 'Choose
what? Women? Women were never that important
to me, Melly, despite what the gossips say. I like
them, enjoy their company, and I don't say I've
never bedded them,' he added with his engaging
grin, 'but not to the degree those same gossips
would have you believe, and the truth of the matter
is I don't feel tied. I enjoy being married to you,
didn't you know that?' he queried lightly.

'Do you?' she smiled, knowing it for the lie it
was.

'Yes, of course. It's also an excuse I can use when
I want to leave somewhere that bores me; an excuse
for importuning women...' With a laugh that
mocked himself, he added more seriously, 'No, the
only regret I have is that I might hurt you. I'm on
a course of self-destruction, Melly, always have
been, you know that. I seem to have this need for
danger; to pit my wits against the world. Constantly
test my abilities. A need to win... I'll make the
best provision I can for you and the child, and then
if anything happens...' With a little shrug, his mood
changed again. 'What shall we do today? Choose
the pram?'

Shaking off her own feeling of despondency that his words had brought, she shook her head. 'No, mustn't tempt fate. I won't choose the pram, or cot, or anything until the last month...'

'But that's ages!' he protested.

'Only eight weeks—it will soon go.'

'I suppose. But I want to *do* things!' he exclaimed comically. 'Get the nursery ready! Choose outfits for him, it, her...'

'Designer?' she asked with a teasing grin.

'Of course designer!' Looking down, he traced an invisible pattern on the tablecloth. 'It frightens me, Melly,' he confessed quietly. 'Being a father. I can't *picture* it. Don't know how I will be.'

'I do,' she said softly. 'You'll be protective, caring—and fun. What more could a child ask?'

'For his father to *be* there, I should think!' With an abrupt move that took her by surprise, he got to his feet. 'I have to go and see someone about the horses. I'll be back in an hour or two; we'll go out then.' Almost at the door, he halted. Turning, he regarded her with a frown. 'Don't you have to go to the clinic today?'

'Mm, but not till two.'

'OK, I'll be back well before that. See you later.' And, with that, he was gone.

Abandoning her attempt to eat, she leaned back and gave an unhappy sigh. Oh, Charles. It was getting harder and harder to appear relaxed, friendly—for him, too, she suspected—but if any intensity was to creep into her voice, any hint of how she felt, she would drive him away. He would feel threatened, and he would leave. She had always known that; she just had not known how desperately hard it would be—or had not wanted to admit it, yet she must have suspected how doomed it would be, with both of them pretending to be something they weren't.

Clenching her hands tight on the napkin, she took slow, deep breaths to let out the tension that his mood had brought. Self-destruction ... He would do the craziest things on a seeming whim: race his yacht; ski down routes that were marked hazardous; stake a fortune on the turn of a card ... And she did not know why, why he had this need to push himself to the limits, punish himself. It wasn't because of Laurent's death, or for making her pregnant; his course of destruction had started long before those two events. Was it because of his upbringing? Because of Beckford? They both had their share of secrets. She didn't know his, and, hopefully, he would never find out hers, for, although he suspected that their meeting wasn't one of those odd coincidences that occurred from time to time, he didn't *know*. Not for certain, not that she had known he was here, and that her desire to visit her grandfather's grave had just been an excuse. A reason for being in the same place as Charles.

Throwing down her napkin, she got awkwardly to her feet and wandered out on to the small terrace. Settling herself in the cushioned chair that Jean-Marc always put out for her, she gazed out over the town spread below.

Charles. He'd coloured her life, given it magic, and every other man paled into insignificance beside him. He was her fantasy, her dream come true. And he had no idea—at least, she hoped he didn't, hoped that he thought she regarded him, as he did her, as an old and valued childhood friend. So, always there must be this need to keep the reins loose, never give him reason to feel trapped, because, without him, life quite simply would not be worth living. She needed him near, and he needed to be free, like a wild horse, but if she was careful, and clever, perhaps he would always come back.

Her eyes unfocused, she thought back to that day over six months before when they had met near the harbour. Correction: when she had engineered the meeting. Although, as in all things, fate had played its part. Had, on that one occasion, played into her hands. And if he found out? No, she thought with a little shudder, he must never find out. He would never understand obsession.

CHAPTER TWO

THERE had been grey skies, a fine drizzle, the day Melly had arrived in France. The overnight ferry had been crowded and she had been glad to reach the relative freedom of the roads. The drive to the Hotel du Golf in Deauville had been without incident, and after unpacking she had wasted no time in gaining directions to the Military Cemetery from the desk clerk. First things first. Set up the alibi.

It was only a five-minute drive from the hotel. A winding road, empty of traffic, then along a small unmarked track, tucked away behind some trees. Isolated. Forgotten? No, not forgotten. All the war graves had been carefully tended. The grass cut.

Shrugging into her slicker, pulling the hood over her dark hair, she climbed from the car. A fitting day for visiting a grave, she thought, with the heavens crying, and guilt was her companion that day, because grandfather's grave was only an excuse. Her father had drawn her a little map, which she had memorised, and, with that in mind, she walked straight to his grave.

Huddling more warmly into her slicker, she gazed before her. Yet, even with her eyes on the grey stone cross, she saw only Charles. Or, said the French way, 'Sharle'. With a small smile, she savoured the name on her tongue. Sharle. No, not here, now; that was a betrayal of them all.

Focusing once more on the memorial stone, she conjured up an image of her grandfather. A face seen only in photographs. A black and white image of a young man that bore a striking resemblance to herself. Mid-brown curly hair, amber eyes with the same wistful expression. And he deserved far more of her attention than she was giving him. He had died for king and country, died so that future generations could be free, and here she was, over forty years later, giving him barely one tenth of her attention.

Captain David Morland. Aged thirty-two.
Liberator.
June 6, 1944

Simple, poignant—and said nothing. How had it really been? Had death come swiftly, on silent wings? Or had it been resisted? Had he known? Or been unaware? There was no one to tell her now. Above the simple inscription was a carving of his regimental badge and his number. Not much as a testament to thirty-two years of life. And yet it was more than some had. Looking round her, at the bleak little cemetery, she shivered and began to move slowly along the row. So young, so little of life had been lived, and she began to silently mouth the names, as though it was important that someone, somewhere, remembered them. Not as a mass, but as individuals.

Most were from the First World War, only a few from the Second. Some were unknown. And in the corner, isolated, were the German war graves. No poignant little messages on these, no soft remembered phrase, just the name and date of death.

Feeling depressed, she turned to go back through the little gate. Duty done. The reason for her trip to France. Liar. With a long sigh, she went back to the car.

Where was Charles now? Still in Deauville? And did she really expect to see him? Yes; the answer had to be yes. Not only expected, but needed. Needed to cure herself of this ridiculous infatuation, because surely that must be what it was? All these years of loving him, wanting him, unable to have a relationship with any other man because it was not him. Yet she *had* tried. Lord knew, she had tried. Accepted invitations from other boys, men, but none of them had had his smile, his warmth, that underlying streak of ruthlessness that sometimes showed in his grey eyes. The strength that could never be disguised. So foolish, irrational—and shaming. Like a schoolgirl languishing after a pop star, an idol. A man who probably rarely gave her a thought, and, if he did, would have been astonished—no, incredulous—had he known of her obsession. Her fantasy.

Putting the car in gear, she drove carefully along the bumpy track and down into the centre of town. People with obsessions always planned well in advance. She had carefully scrutinised the town map and therefore knew exactly where the harbour was. Knew, or at least had been told, that that was where Charles moored his yacht.

Finding the marina without difficulty, she parked, and then quickly scanned the line of expensive toys as they bobbed gently, swayed, curtsied, as if in mockery. And there it was, exactly like the photograph she had seen in the magazine

at home. The *Wanderer*. Elegant, racy, exciting—
like the man who stood on deck. An unexpected
bonus, and she felt the familiar warmth course
through her as she stared at dark hair ruffled by
the breeze; at strong, tanned arms that were raised
as he fiddled with something on the mast; at jeans-
clad legs, astride to keep his balance. Slim, elegant,
exciting. Charles Revington.

She stared at him for a long time, felt the jolt
she always felt; felt her heart race, swell, and she
wanted to do something incredibly juvenile, such
as walk past him in the hope that he might see her.

Wrenching her eyes away, she was disgusted by
her stupidity. And it was stupid, and childish, and
hopeless. Climbing from the car, she quickly locked
it, and, resolutely turning her back, she began to
walk along the wooden promenade that divided the
long sandy beach from the bathing huts.

'Hey! Melly! Hang on!'

If you wanted something badly enough you
would get it. Closing her eyes tight for a moment,
she quickened her step, pretended she had not heard
the urgent shout. Staring blindly at the wooden
boards before her, she fought for composure. Fool.
Stop, be casual. I can't. The longing to see him and
the need to escape were equally powerful. She
should never have come. And yet, if it was he who
chased after her, it would look, wouldn't it, as
though their meeting was accidental?

The sound of footsteps behind her did not dim-
inish, and it was almost a relief when her arm was
caught and she was brought to a halt. Swinging
round in feigned surprise, she stared up into the
face of the man she had loved since she was a child.

Laughing grey eyes looked back. A wide smile stretched the firm tanned skin of his face. 'I would have felt the most awful fool if it hadn't been you! What on earth is my innocent little friend doing in this den of iniquity?' he asked with that engaging grin that had been haunting her for most of her twenty-five years.

'Oh, this and that,' she managed simply. Surprised, after all, at how easy it was, she smiled. Her heart might be racing, her pulse erratic, but, to her intense relief, she sounded ordinary, normal. 'Hello, Charles.'

' "Hello, Charles," ' he mimicked lightly. 'So casual, Melly? You don't even sound surprised.'

Cursing herself for not at least pretending, she fabricated. 'Not surprised, no; more—disbelieving, I think. I certainly didn't expect to see anyone I knew.'

'No,' he agreed gently, 'that's what's so nice about travelling. One never knows who one will bump into.' And, sounding as though he really meant it, he added, 'It's really good to see you.' His eyes full of devilish laughter, he grasped her shoulders and kissed her smoothly on each cheek, then before she could register the feel of him, the warmth, he steered her towards the only nearby café that was open. In the summer, she guessed, the wide glass panels would be pushed back, and tables and chairs would be placed outside, but today, in early April, and with a cold east wind blowing, they were mostly all closed and shuttered.

Hooking a chair out with his foot, he pushed her gently into the seat before taking the chair opposite. Summoning the waiter with an ease that she envied, he quirked an eyebrow in query. 'Coffee?'

'Please, white.'

'Deux cafés-crème, s'il vous plaît.'

'Grands? Petits?' the waiter asked smoothly.

'Grands, merci.'

As soon as the waiter had departed to execute their order, he continued, 'So what brings you to Deauville? Not the racing,' he teased, 'that doesn't start till August. The golf? The sailing? The casino?'

Settling back in her chair, not quite sure she believed this was happening, and that Charles was actually sitting opposite her, a quizzical expression on his strong face, she toyed idly with a sugar wrapper someone had left on the table. Even though hope had been warring with expectancy, she still found it hard to believe that her fantasising, her irrational hopes, were being realised. Glancing up at him, she felt faint. 'Not the casino, no. The war graves.'

'The war... Oh.' With a nod of understanding, he slapped the table. 'Of course, your grandfather. You're looking for his grave?' Noting her astonishment, he smiled. 'I remember your father once telling me that his father had fought and died in Normandy during the D-Day landings. Any luck?'

'Yes. I knew, of course, that it was the Military Cemetery at Tourgeville; it was just a question of finding it. The authorities were very helpful when I contacted them in England—they even offered to take me there.'

'But you wanted to go alone,' he put in understandingly.

'Yes. I've just come from there.'

'Which is why you're looking so pensive,' he exclaimed softly, 'and insensitive Charles Revington has just trampled all over your feelings with his size-nine boots. I'm sorry.'

With a renewed stab of guilt, because she hadn't been feeling any of the emotions he expected of her, she protested softly, 'No need to be sorry, and insensitive is the last thing I'd call you. I was just feeling a little sad, and thoughtful, I suppose.'

With a gentle hand he removed the wrapper from her fingers, then lifted them to his mouth and kissed the tips. '*Triste*. That's what the French would say. Have you been to look at the landing beaches? Sword, Juno, Gold, Omaha?'

'No, not yet.' No need to tell him that she had only arrived that morning.

'You should make the time. They're worth seeing, and the American Cemetery in Saint Laurent. It will bring a lump to your throat. So many crosses, so many dead.'

'Yes, I will.' With a little smile for the waiter, and a hesitant, '*Merci*,' she gratefully turned her attention to putting sugar in her coffee and stirring it. He was too near, too charming, too much the man, and she could think of nothing to say, nothing that would interest him. From longing for the chance to see him, talk to him, now that the moment was here she felt gauche, shy, uninteresting.

'You're on your own?'

'Yes.'

'Then the least I can do is buy you dinner...'

'Oh, no!' she exclaimed in sudden panic. 'Truly, you don't need to do that.'

'I know I don't,' he agreed with another teasing smile, 'but I would like to. You can tell me all that's been happening at home. You still live in Beckford? That good old hotbed of gossip?'

Feeling unworldly and suburban, she gave a wry smile and nodded.

'Still at home?' he teased.

Wishing she could invent a worldly lifestyle for herself, suddenly transpose into an exciting, intriguing companion, she gave another reluctant nod. 'Very unenterprising of me, I know, but, well, I'm quite happy there.'

'No need to sound defensive, or apologetic,' he said gently, 'we can't all be adventurers.' With a wry smile of his own, he picked up his cup. 'Still the wicked one, am I?' he queried with a crooked grin.

''Fraid so. Unredeemable. They're all just waiting for your sticky end so that they can say ''I told you so'' to each other.' Studying him while his attention was elsewhere, she wondered if he minded. He didn't look as though he did, but then, Charles never looked anything but amused. It had been nearly fifteen years since he had actually lived in the village, and, although she had seen him from time to time, when he had made a flying visit to Beckford for her brother's funeral, returned quite often to see old friends, it had been over a year since she had last seen him, and then only briefly, and from a distance, which perhaps was why she had felt this overwhelming need to see him now. 'You no longer go back?' She knew very well he didn't, knew that his old friends had moved away, but she didn't want him to know that she knew.

Didn't want him to know of her infatuation. Her obsessive interest in his affairs.

Returning his attention to her, he gave a faint smile and shook his head. 'Still writing your children's books?'

'Yes, still doing them.'

'No more yearnings to be a nurse?' he asked with a quizzical smile.

'No,' she denied with a faint grin as she remembered that youthful ambition, remembered his teasing.

'Well, if determination should win any prizes you'd get the big one. Still unpublished?'

'No,' she denied with a touch of pride. 'I am now, well, if not exactly rich and famous, at least being sold.'

Looking genuinely pleased, he exclaimed, 'Congratulations! What name do you write under? Would I have heard of you?'

Amused, she shook her head. 'I doubt it.'

'Tell me anyway,' he persuaded gently, and as though he really was interested. But then, that was part of his charm, he always appeared interested in other people's doings.

Knowing he would make the connection, she confessed reluctantly, 'Donny.'

'Ah.' With a sympathetic nod, he said, 'For your brother.'

'Yes.'

'Your parents have come to terms with it now?'

'On the surface perhaps, but inside? No, not really,' she said with rather haunting sadness.

'Is that why you stayed at home?' he asked gently.

'Partly, I suppose. Whenever I made noises about leaving, finding a flat, they didn't exactly say anything, but they looked so hurt that I didn't have the heart to persist.'

'Kind Melissa.'

With a little shrug, she finished her coffee. She wasn't sure kind came into it. Cowardice perhaps, or guilt. Not that she really had anything to feel guilty for, and yet, whenever she had broached the subject about leaving, guilt was what they had made her feel. And if she had left, lived a different sort of life, would she have got over this need for Charles? And yet, to be honest, mostly, she didn't feel a desperate need to try her wings elsewhere, just now and again when she began to feel stifled by the feelings of responsibility her parents engendered in her. There was also the question of money. Due to the fact that her father had lost all interest in his business when Donny had died, their income now was quite small, and without her contribution they would have found it hard to manage. So she stayed, and if her brother's ghost was part of the package, well, it was an amiable ghost, not one that ever threatened her peace of mind. She could think of him now with love and affection, not the aching pain that his death had brought over ten years before. Such a silly death, such a wasteful, foolish way to die, to trip and knock yourself out and then drown in a puddle barely big enough to wet your shoes.

Pushing the memories aside, she asked lightly, 'So what are you up to these days? Apart from being an adventurer, that is?'

'Oh, this and that,' he dismissed. 'I get by.'

She could see that, she thought wryly, if the sailing jacket he was wearing was anything to go by. That certainly hadn't come from Woolworths. But any chance to probe further was thwarted by the appearance of a woman who seemed vaguely familiar. She was tall, and fair, and very, very attractive, and her face was full of laughter and lively curiosity as she stared at Melly through the window behind Charles. Putting a finger to her lips to indicate silence, she slipped in through the door, tiptoed across to the table, and then put both hands over Charles's eyes.

Grasping her wrists in his strong hands, he removed them and turned to peer upwards, then grinned. *'Bonjour, madame,'* he greeted lightly.

'I'll give you *"bonjour"*! You are a wretched, wretched man, Charles! Where have you been? And why didn't you come to my party?'

'I was busy,' he drawled laconically, and Melly got the definite feeling that those narrowed grey eyes held a warning. For the woman not to presume, perhaps? This was a part of him that she had never seen, and just for a moment she felt a little *frisson* of fear at her temerity in seeking him out. He was not a boy, but a man of the world, sophisticated, wealthy. In his own setting he was vastly different from her childhood friend.

'Yes, and I can imagine what with!' the woman laughed, bringing Melly back to the present with a start.

'I'm sure you can.'

With a comical grimace, and a little smile for Melly, she hurried to rejoin her companions outside.

What had he been busy with? Melly wondered as she followed the elegant blonde's progress with her eyes. Women? His yacht? Not something she could ask. Finally turning back to face him, she observed, 'She looks a bit like the actress...'

'Alison Marks,' he put in coolly. 'Yes. She is.'

'Hm,' she offered ruefully. 'You move in exalted circles.'

'Exalted?' he queried thoughtfully. 'No, they're just ordinary people. Quite nice, some of them. You should come back in September; they're all here then for the film festival.' Seeing her puzzlement, he clarified, 'The American Film Festival. It's held in Deauville each year. Want to go? I'll get tickets for you if you like.'

'Me? Good heavens, no!' she denied without really thinking about it.

'Sure? I can get you an invite. Rub shoulders with the rich and famous... No, perhaps not,' he added softly with a little shake of his head. 'A lamb among lions...' With another, more genuine smile, he continued, 'It would probably bore you to tears. Not your sort of people, Melly. All full of their own egos.'

Which, of course, perversely, made her want to change her mind, a fact he very well knew, judging by the twinkle in his eyes.

The crashing open of the door made them both turn. A man with grey hair and a weatherbeaten face was standing in the opening, and he stared at Charles with an expression of almost despair on his face.

'*Qu'est-ce qu'il y a?*' Charles queried with a frown.

A burst of French issued from the other man, and the only word Melly caught was a name, Laurent.

Shoving his chair back, Charles hurried across to the man standing agitatedly in the doorway, and Melly didn't need to be able to understand French to know that Charles was demanding details of whatever it was that had happened.

Quickly finding some francs, she put them on the table to pay for the coffee, then, pushing her own chair back, she hurried to join the two men who were striding urgently back towards the harbour. Something was wrong, that was obvious, but what?

There was a large knot of people on the quay, all talking, obviously discussing whatever it was that had occurred, and she watched Charles and his companion stride up to some sort of official and begin to question him. She saw him nod, then shove his hands into his pockets and look out towards the open sea.

She could have gone away then, left quietly, without fuss, because she knew he'd forgotten all about her, but she didn't want to go away, didn't want to leave. Moving to stand beside him, she asked hesitantly, 'Is something wrong?'

Snapping his head round, and then staring at her as though he wasn't sure who she was, he gave a long shudder, and with an obvious effort focused his attention on her.

'Melly. Oh, hell, I'm sorry...'

'Don't be ridiculous, tell me what's happened.'

'It's Laurent—well, Laurent's yacht, at any rate; apparently a motor cruiser went into her side. I don't know any details; the rescue launch has gone out...' Breaking off, he continued, more to himself than her, 'He'll be all right. More lives than a cat...' And then he closed his eyes, as if he was silently praying.

'Charles,' his companion said quietly and, grasping his arm, drew his attention to the rescue launch that was slowly entering the harbour. Glancing at Charles's face, she saw hope warring with bleak presentiment. Averting her eyes, she too stared at the launch as it slowly motored to the quayside.

A man and a woman were escorted off first, the woman weeping hysterically, the man white and obviously shaken. No one else, only the blue uniformed figures. Charles and his companion walked towards the man who was obviously in charge. She saw him shake his head.

Feeling helpless, and useless, she watched as a white-shrouded form was stretchered up and put carefully on the cobbles. Saw Charles kneel and gently pull back the covering to stare down at, presumably, the face of his friend, and then stand helplessly by as the stretcher was picked up and carried to the waiting ambulance. The other man accompanied it, leaving Charles looking lost and anguished, unbearably hurt.

Her heart aching for him, she walked back to his side. Slipping her hand into his arm, she held it warmly against her.

'I should have gone with him,' he said bleakly. 'I was intending to, only I wanted to finish fixing something on *Wanderer*. If I'd been with him...'

'If you'd gone with him,' she said gently, 'it might have been you.'

'You think that matters? No, Melly, it wouldn't have mattered at all. No loss to anyone. But Laurent . . . Oh, God.' Turning his head, and obviously becoming aware of the knots of people still talking, speculating, he clenched his teeth and eyes tight for a moment, then, grasping her hand, he said harshly, 'Let's get out of here before the Press arrive!'

Pulling her along the sandy track and across the main road towards a block of flats, he pushed through the main entrance door and into a waiting lift. Pressing the button for the third floor, he kept his face resolutely turned to one side, away from her, until the lift halted and the door slid open.

Melly had just time enough to notice that the landing was covered with expensive green carpet, the walls painted cream, before she was tugged along to a door at the end. Flat three hundred and one. Charles inserted his key and, still grasping her hand, pulled her inside. Releasing her, he strode along the tiny hall and into a door at the end. Following slowly, she watched him push open the french windows of the large square lounge and step out on to the balcony for a brief moment. Then, still without speaking, he came inside and made for the bar set up in one corner.

Feeling totally inadequate, and uncertain what to do for the best, she investigated the kitchen and made coffee and sandwiches, neither of which Charles touched, but just refilled his glass every time it was empty and stood staring out over the harbour. Knowing there was nothing she could say to alleviate his suffering, she thought it was probably best to allow him to come to terms with it in his own way. Curling up in the armchair, she watched and waited, in case he should need something. Anything. A shoulder to lean on, cry on. Someone to hold.

As the sky gradually purpled, then blackened, he gave a long sigh and gently pushed the windows to. Turning, he stared at her for a moment before walking, quite steadily, across to the standard lamp and switching it on.

'Thank you,' he said simply. 'I'll be all right.'

'Yes,' she agreed helplessly.

Walking across to the cream leather sofa, he sat, still nursing his glass, and began to talk. All about Laurent, their friendship, the things they had done together. 'He was my friend,' he concluded quietly. 'My very good friend.' A look of such agony crossed his face that Melly felt tears start to her eyes. Placing his glass carefully on the floor, he hunched over, his head on his knees. Without stopping to think, she rose quickly, and sat beside him. Putting her arms round him, she held him close, laid her head against his and rocked him silently.

'Don't go,' he said thickly.

'No, I'll be here. As long as you need me to stay, I'll be here.'

They had sat for a long time like that, until, eventually, she had helped him into his bedroom, helped him undress, and had then lain beside him in silent comfort.

*   *   *

'*Madame*? *Madame*!'

With a little start, she blinked, turning her head, and stared rather blankly at Jean-Marc.

'It is the telephone, *madame*. Your mother.'

'Mother? Oh, right, thank you.'

Feeling disorientated and muzzy, she got reluctantly to her feet. Memories of that night spent with Charles remained vivid in her mind and, for a moment, she was resentful at having to put them aside. Memories of his lovemaking would probably be all she ever had. All she maybe deserved, because she had made a conscious decision to stay with him that night. It hadn't only been the action of a friend; it had also been a selfish desire to be near him. With a little sad sigh, she followed Jean-Marc inside.

CHAPTER THREE

AFTER a really rather pointless conversation with her mother, and reassuring her that she felt fine, and yes, would let her know the results of her scan, Melly replaced the receiver. Poor mother, stuck over in England while her one remaining, and very pregnant, chick lived in France. She was still trying to persuade Melly to go to England to have the baby. She didn't trust the French; didn't think they had decent hospitals; thought the food was bad for her; and, as always, Melly soothed her, explained yet again that French hospitals were probably better than English ones; that the food was fine, didn't upset her, knowing full well that her mother's anti-French feelings were just an excuse. It was Charles she didn't trust. She had also been angling for another invitation, and, naughtily, Melly had pretended not to notice. She had already been out twice, and Melly didn't think Charles would be too pleased at another visit quite so soon. Neither, if she was honest, would she. Mother would fuss, organise, send her to bed; make her put her feet up; and would again comment on the fact that she and Charles didn't share a room. And her poor father, who Mother always insisted accompany her, would wander round, looking lost and uncomfortable, fervently wishing he could go home and back to his small engineering workshop where he could hide from the world.

'Mother?' Charles queried humorously from behind her.

Turning in surprise, she smiled. 'Yes. I didn't hear you come in.'

'When's she coming?' he asked with rueful acceptance.

'She isn't. Or, at least, not yet...' Laughing, she added, 'It's all right, you can say it!'

'*Moi*?' he asked with a grin. 'I'm much too polite. However...'

'Quite.' Still smiling, she queried, 'Have any luck in finding a new stable?'

With a friendly arm round her shoulder, he steered her into the lounge and seated her on the sofa before collapsing beside her. 'No, the owner and I had a long talk, and I decided, after much deliberation, to leave them where they are.'

'Because?' she asked lightly. She knew this husband of hers well enough to know that, if the owner had a problem, financial or otherwise, and unloaded it on to Charles, Charles would immediately set about finding a solution, and therefore wouldn't dream of adding to his troubles by taking his horses away. Unless of course it was the owner's mismanagement, or laziness, that had created the problem; then it would have been a very different story.

'Oh,' he dismissed, 'he's had one or two problems... Why are you laughing?'

'No reason,' she denied with a fond smile, 'go on.'

'Nothing to go on with. I just decided to leave them with him for the time being. Anyway, with the racing season finished, there's no immediate hurry. So, want to go out for lunch before your hospital appointment?'

Knowing it was what he wanted, she nodded. 'Love to. Where shall we go?'

'Ciros?'

'Great. Will we get in?' She knew very well that, with the town still crammed to capacity after the film festival, restaurant bookings were like gold dust.

'Of course.'

'Of course,' she laughed, and wondered not for the first time what levers he used in order to get a table when no one else could. 'I'll go and get ready.'

They were welcomed as Charles was welcomed everywhere, with delight, with a grin and with excellent service. He explained to the head waiter that she was to have a scan that afternoon, and would therefore need to drink at least one and a half pints of liquid. Not an eyelid was batted, not a comment made, and she was smilingly presented with a large carafe of water, and one of orange juice. Charles watched her with smiling concern as she battled to drink the required amount without once going to the ladies'.

'God, I'm glad I'm not a woman!' he exclaimed fervently when they were ready to leave. 'Is it really necessary to drink all that?'

'So they say. Apparently the scan won't work properly otherwise. Don't ask me why, because I don't know. I did ask,' she added comically, 'but I didn't understand the answer.'

Hugging her to his side, he kept his arm round her as he escorted her back to the car.

*   *   *

The scan itself went off without difficulty; it was when she returned to the reception desk for her card, after a hasty visit to the ladies', that the troubles began.

'Ah, Madame Revington,' the receptionist said, and then, presumably remembering that Melly was English, proudly displayed her talent in that direction. 'Dr Lafage,' she enunciated slowly, 'he is wishing to see you. *Oui*?' she asked triumphantly.

'*Oui, très bien*,' Melly complimented. 'Where? And, more importantly, why?' she asked lightly. 'I didn't have to see him before.' Registering the woman's total incomprehension, she gave a wry smile, and because she couldn't be bothered to dredge up her shaky French she turned to Charles, and silently asked him to translate for her. Which he did with a fluency she envied. He would only intercede if she asked, because he said the only way for her to learn the language fluently was to practise on every conceivable occasion. Which was true, she thought wryly, but it made life very complicated sometimes.

'She doesn't know why,' Charles informed her with a smile. 'Probably just routine.' Thanking the receptionist, he collected Melly's notes and, with a hand solicitously beneath her elbow, escorted her down to the antenatal clinic.

Dr Lafage saw them straight away. Another one who spoke English, which only went to emphasise how lazy the English were at learning foreign languages.

'*Madame, m'sieu*,' he smiled, 'please be seated. Now, we would like for you to go on the monitor. Yes? You have been on it before, I understand.'

Consulting the notes that Charles had given him, he nodded. 'Yes, last month.' Leaning back in his chair, he beamed at her. 'Tell me how you are feeling. You have backache, perhaps? Headaches?'

'No. Cramp sometimes, heartburn; other that that, I feel fine.'

'No dizziness? Faintness?'

'No.'

'*Bien*. You are eating properly?'

'Yes.'

'Taking the tablets for the iron and vitamin?'

'Yes,' she agreed a little impatiently. 'Is there some problem?'

'Well, we hope not. Are almost sure not, but...'

Beginning to feel more and more alarmed, she sought Charles's hand and then held it tight. 'But?'

With a long sigh, he explained, 'Your blood-pressure is a little high—nothing to get alarmed about, just a little higher than we would like. And it might be best if we had you in for a few days, just to be on the side of safe...'

'But if it's only a little bit high...'

'It is true, it is not a matter for too much concern, but we would like for you to rest.'

'I do rest! And, if I need to rest more, I will!' she insisted. Her face reflecting her worry, she asked faintly, 'There's nothing wrong with the baby, is there?'

'*Non*! *Non*, the baby is fine...'

'Then why? If the baby is fine...'

'It is fine; please, you must not get distressed. It is only that we have the minor concern that it is small, not growing as fast as we would like. There is nothing to worry about, but we would like to put you on the monitor, just for safety's sake for half of the hour, and then, if that is all right, which I'm sure it will be,' he reassured hastily, 'you may go home. But next week we would like you to come for another scan.' Getting to his feet, he waited until they stood and then walked round the desk to escort them to the door. Smiling down at her, he patted her shoulder. 'Don't worry, all will be well, I'm sure.'

Then why say anything at all? she wondered. Searching his face as he opened the door and beckoned to a passing nurse, trying to see if there was something he wasn't telling her, she turned to her husband. 'Charles?' she asked helplessly.

Taking her face between his palms, he smiled down at her. 'Stop worrying and do as the doctor says. You go with the nurse; I'll have a chat with him, find out what I can. Go on, I'll come along and find you in a minute.'

Nodding, she gave the nurse a worried smile, and accompanied her along to one of the cubicles. Obediently climbing on to the bed, she lay back. What did the doctor mean, small? How small? And what did he mean about not growing? The nurse, unfortunately, didn't speak English, and all the French Melly had ever known had flown out of her head. All she could remember was how to ask for the pen of her aunt. The damned stupid things they taught you in school. She could conceive of no situation whatsoever when anyone might need to ask for the pen of their aunt! Why couldn't they teach you useful things? Like how to ask about small babies? Giving an agitated little sigh, she tried to relax. Getting worked up might affect the baby's heartbeat, which would be picked up by the monitor, and then they would keep her in.

With her tummy exposed and the monitor strapped in place, Melly had nothing to do but listen to the sound of her baby's heart and watch the numbers jump erratically on the crystal display. The nurse watched them for a moment, nodded as though satisfied, adjusted the paper strip that interpreted the numbers on to a print-out graph, gave Melly's leg a reassuring pat and left.

Forcing herself to stay calm, she kept her eyes fixed on the numbers, willing them to stay normal. So long as the baby's heart is beating, everything's all right, she told herself firmly. So who cares if it's a small baby? Small babies do fine, better sometimes than larger ones, but what did the doctor mean about its not growing as it should? Not forming properly? Is that what he meant?

Hearing Charles's voice just outside the cubicle as he spoke to the nurse, she relaxed and sank back. Charles would make sure everything was all right.

'You look like one of Frankenstein's experiments,' he commented with a grin as he pushed through the curtain.

'It's what I feel like. What did the doctor say?'

'Not much more than he said to you.' Walking to the side of the bed, he picked up her hand and held it comfortingly between his own. 'I don't think there's any need to get worried,' he said gently, 'they're just being careful.'

'Yes,' she agreed gratefully. 'But you would tell me if it was anything——'

'I promise. Now——'

'But did you ask him what he meant by the baby's not growing? Supposing it's not——'

'Melly!' he interrupted. 'Everything's going to be fine! Now, tell me what all this gadgetry is for.'

'You know what it's for! You were here when they explained it all last time.'

'I've forgotten,' he said blandly.

She knew he hadn't, but talking would take her mind off her worries, and if Charles wasn't concerned... 'The display on the left is the baby's heartbeat, the one on the right is mine.'

'And the print-out is confirmation that all is OK,' he said confidently. Patting her hand, he released it and walked round to stare at the paper being spewed from the machine.

'It looks very erratic,' she ventured nervously.

'So would you be if you were a tiny baby and that cold disc was plonked right on top of you,' he said with a smile as he indicated the plate attached to her stomach. 'Stop worrying!'

'Yes. I just wish——'

'That the doctor wouldn't go around scaremongering!' he said forcefully. 'I know! Damned fool!'

Diverted, she asked curiously, 'Did you tell him so?'

'Of course,' he retorted with an aloof certainty that he would always be listened to.

'What did he say?'

Turning to look at her, he suddenly relaxed and smiled. Spreading his hands and shrugging his shoulders, presumably as the doctor had done, he parodied, '"*M'sieu*, I am devastated. It was not my wish to concern your lovely wife! It is only that the most current policy is to explain all to the new mother-to-be! Women insist on it!'' He then said something that sounded like ''Pshaw'', and gave a long discourse on how things have changed and that everything was much better in the old days. And if he doesn't very speedily revert to the ''old ways'',' he disparaged arrogantly, 'and give you the care and attention I think you should have, he will very speedily find himself being replaced!'

And that, she knew, was not an idle threat, and she doubted the doctor would make the mistake of underestimating him again. Before their marriage, and from what she knew of him, she had always assumed that Charles didn't get annoyed, or involved, not because he couldn't, but because he didn't want to. She had thought that he liked life to be smooth and without aggravation. And maybe he did, but that didn't prevent him arrogantly overruling anyone if he thought the occasion demanded it. And such was his standing in the community, and the awe in which people seemed to hold him, that he invariably got his way. That *had* surprised her, perhaps because in Beckford he was generally regarded as a lightweight. Kind, charming, but without depth; but that was very far from the truth, as she had very speedily discovered. So, either he had changed radically over the years, or he had always been like it and she had just never seen it. From feeling youthful devotion, which she now knew had been based in fantasy, she had grown to love him with an intensity that frightened her. And if he had truly been a lightweight she doubted now that her love would have survived. Without her realising it, perhaps, she too had grown up.

With a thoughtful frown she lay back again and watched as he prowled round the small room, picking up literature, glancing through it, grimacing comically and replacing it in the rack. Always fearful of his becoming bored, or irritated, and therefore marring the smooth life she was trying to build for them both, she persuaded softly, 'Why don't you go and get a cup of coffee?'

'Hm?' Glancing round at her, he only slowly registered what she had said, and a small smile tugged at the corner of his mouth. Walking across to her, he reproved gently, 'It's from a *machine*, Melly. And if you had ever tasted it you would not wish it on your worst enemy, let alone me!'

Laughing, she held her hand out to him. 'Thank you for coming with me today.'

'And what else should I do?' he asked gently as he came to sit on the edge of the bed. 'You're my wife, and,' placing one large palm gently on the part of her stomach that wasn't covered by the monitor, he continued, 'this is my baby. Of course I would come. I wonder what it is? Lauren, or Laurent?'

She had asked, when they were first married, if he would like the baby to be named after his friend who had died. Lauren if it was a girl, and Laurent if it was a boy. He had seemed almost overwhelmed. Smiling at him, she teased, 'So long as it isn't one of each.'

'Oh, hell. No, it would have shown up on the scan—wouldn't it?'

'Probably,' she comforted. She didn't care what it was, or how many it was, so long as everything was all right.

Turning back to watch the monitor, he continued thoughtfully, 'I read somewhere that, if the heartbeat stays under forty, it's a boy. Over, it's a girl.' With a wide smile he watched the monitor jump from thirty-eight to fifty and then back down to thirty-six. 'Perhaps it hasn't made up its mind yet,' he commented humorously. 'It doesn't seem to stay either above or below.'

'It had better——' Breaking off as the nurse came in, Melly carefully watched her face as she stopped the machine and tore off the graph.

Turning, she gave Melly a wide smile. 'Is OK,' she said triumphantly. Whether for her English, or the graph, Melly wasn't sure, but she didn't miss the flirtatious glance she gave Charles.

He asked her something in French, and the nurse replied, and, to Melly's heightened imagination, seemed to linger over what she wanted to say. It was Charles who broke the contact by standing and saying something very softly to the young nurse. She blushed scarlet and hastily unstrapped Melly from the machine.

Charles rearranged her maternity dress over her bulge and helped her to her feet. 'We can go home. All, as the nurse said, is OK. You are to come back next Wednesday.'

Hitching her dress into a more comfortable position and collecting her bag, she asked quietly, 'What did you say to make the nurse blush?'

Bending his head to drop a light kiss on her hair, he said softly, 'I told her to behave herself, that I was a happily married man.'

And are you? she wanted to ask as they walked out to his car. Are you happy? Or are you just acting out a role? That of a devoted husband and father-to-be? You were the one who settled for the crumbs, she told herself with an inward sigh; don't complain now that they aren't enough.

'Come on, upstairs,' he insisted when they got home, 'the doctor said you were to rest. And we'll stay in this evening,' he added as he helped her on to the bed.

'No,' she put in softly. 'We'll go out, as planned. It's only a dinner party, not standing around or anything, and it will help take my mind off things. if I stay in I'll only lie and worry.'

Staring down at her for a moment, he frowned, then finally nodded. 'All right, but only for a little while. We won't stay late.' Slipping off her shoes, he pulled the quilt across her and tucked it warmly at her side. Perching on the edge of the bed, he smoothed her unruly hair back with a gentle hand. 'Get some sleep. I'll give you a knock about seven.'

'All right—and Charles?' she called softly as he got up and walked to the door. 'Thank you.'

'Nothing to thank me for, Melly,' he denied rather sombrely. 'Nothing at all.'

A light tickle on her nose woke her, and with a little twitch she opened her eyes. Charles was sitting on the edge of the bed, a small white feather in his hand.

'I found it when I was out for a walk,' he said with a faint smile. 'A tickling feather. How do you feel?'

'Fine.' I'd be even finer if I could reach up my arms, pull you close, kiss you. 'Fine,' she repeated, and forced herself to smile.

'I've been thinking,' he continued thoughtfully as he continued to stare rather absently at her.

'What about?'

'You, me. Have I seemed a reluctant husband to you, Melly? No, don't answer that; I know I have. After I left you I went for a long walk, just wandered round, thinking, and I discovered, to my surprise, that I actually quite like being married to you. That I like coming home to find you here; and, because it's a feeling that has crept over me gradually, I didn't immediately realise it. But today, at the hospital, when the doctor spouted all that rubbish, I suddenly thought how much I would miss you if you were no longer around. I think I've tended to forget that it isn't only I who's had to change. So I'm sorry if I've been selfish, or unkind.'

'You haven't,' she insisted, her voice thick, choked.

'Haven't I?' With a quirky smile, he tossed the feather on to the bedside table. 'It hasn't been easy for either of us, has it? Both circling round warily, afraid perhaps to be ourselves. You've felt it too, I know—because I do *not* recall, back in Beckford, that you were ever this meek!'

'No,' she agreed cautiously.

'So, what I'm trying to say is, shall we try being ourselves? You're not unhappy here, are you?'

'No. I'm very happy here.' I could be happier, but...

'Good.'

'Are you?' she asked quietly.

'Me?' he asked in surprise, as though no one had ever asked him that before. 'Yes, I just told you.

I've been thinking, too, that maybe it's time I changed, became a proper businessman...'

'You are a proper businessman, and I don't want you to change. I like you fine just as you are.' Did he think she didn't know how hard he worked? That his playboy image was just that? An image? Or did he think she didn't care? So long as he kept her in a certain lifestyle? No, surely he couldn't think that?

'Do you?' As he glanced at her his smile widened, became mischievous. 'Then shall we try?'

Nodding, her eyes still a trifle wary, she was startled when he leaned down and put his head on her shoulder. Lifting his legs, he lay beside her on the bed. 'You inside the cover,' he commented humorously, 'me outside. Will it always be that way?' he added quietly.

Not sure what he meant, she lay very still, and could only hope he meant what it sounded as though he meant. 'Do you want it to stay that way?' she asked carefully.

'No.' Flicking his eyes up to hers, he gave a slow grin. 'It's funny, I always thought of myself as a loner, and now I can't imagine life without you. You're a very soothing sort of person, Melly. You make the house seem like home.' With a gentle hand he turned her face towards him. 'But we'll wait until after the baby's born, shall we? Just to be on the safe side. I can wait that long—I think,' he added comically. 'Although, in the meantime...' Stretching sideways, he claimed her mouth, and, with a little mumbled sound of satisfaction, continued to kiss her with slow enjoyment. As he lifted his head his eyes smiled into hers. With what sounded like a contented sigh, he put his head back on her shoulder and rested his arm carefully across her stomach. 'This is nice.' Closing his eyes, he gave every appearance of a man composing himself for sleep.

'Charles,' she exclaimed with a shaky little laugh, 'we're supposed to be going out!'

Nuzzling into her side, he mumbled, 'Mmmm.'

'Don't you want to go out?'

'No.' Rolling on to his back, he spread his arms wide. 'But I suppose we'd better. I have to see Sebastien about something. Property matter,' he added vaguely. Turning his head towards her, he smiled again. 'Best get ready, then, hm?'

'I guess so.'

With a little nod he got lithely to his feet. 'OK. I'll get Jean-Marc to make us a light snack. See you downstairs.' With a little waggle of his fingers, he went out and along to his own room.

Did he mean what she thought he meant? With a little flutter of excitement she held her arms protectively across her tummy. Dear God, I hope so, she prayed fervently. To have a proper marriage— that was something she hadn't dared to dream about. Putting her fingers to her lips, which still tingled from his touch, she closed her eyes in order to better savour the memory of his kiss. She wanted more. So much more... And when the baby was born? Not daring to hope in case fate snatched it away, she rolled to her feet and went to get ready.

When she'd showered and made up her face she opened the wide doors of her wardrobe to survey the contents. She had any number of smart maternity dresses that Charles had bought for her, even though she had insisted it was a waste of money, that she would never get to wear all of them, but when Charles got a bee in his bonnet he refused to be thwarted, so here they all were. Rifling slowly along the rail, she picked out a dress in navy silk. Slipping it over her head, she had to admit that it felt good. Looked good, despite the bulge. Bending to take out the matching shoes from the bottom, she gasped and bit her lip as a sharp pain shot through her stomach.

It's all right, it's all right, it's only cramp, she told herself. Cramp, that's all. You've had it before; no need to get paranoid just because the doctor said those dumb things earlier. Cautiously straightening, she waited a moment, but when the pain didn't return she slowly took a deep, relaxing breath. It was all right; she felt fine. Placing one hand on her stomach, she smiled in relief when she felt the baby kick.

'Melly?' Charles called softly through the door.

'Come in, I'm almost ready.' Slipping her feet into her shoes, she turned away to pick up her evening bag. 'Right, I'm ready,' she said brightly as she turned back to face him.

He was watching her, his eyes slightly narrowed. 'What's wrong?' he asked quietly.

'Wrong? Nothing.'

'Don't lie to me, Melly,' he continued in the same soft voice. 'Something's upset you. What?'

'Nothing. Truly, it's nothing,' she insisted. Smiling, she walked across and laid her hand on his arm. 'Truly. Just a touch of cramp. It's gone now.'

'Sure?'

'Positive.'

'We can stay in——'

'No. I'm fine now; please don't fuss. Besides, it's only a dinner party, and, as you said, I will be sitting down.' With another smile, she lifted her hand and smoothed the material of his lapel. 'You look very smart.' More than smart, she mentally qualified. Devastating. His dinner jacket was of impeccable cut, fitted him like a glove. No creases, wrinkles, just a superb fit.

The concern in his eyes replaced by a twinkle, he bowed his head in silent thanks. 'I might have to call in at the casino,' he explained, 'hence the dinner jacket. You won't mind? It will only be for a few minutes.'

'Liar,' she teased softly. 'Bring me home first, then you can go with a quiet mind.'

'Ah, you know me so well.' Holding his arm out to her, he waited until she'd slipped her hand in the crook of his elbow before walking towards the door. 'Your carriage awaits, my lady.'

Fabienne opened the door to them. Presumably because she had seen them arriving and wanted to be the first to greet Charles, Melly thought uncharitably.

'Darling!' she exclaimed theatrically. The polite kiss on each cheek became a passionate embrace when initiated by Fabienne, and Melly clenched her hands tight by her sides. It would hardly get the evening off to a good start if she attacked their hostess, as she wanted very much to do. Continuing to ignore Melly, she drew Charles inside in a deliberate attempt to part them. She didn't succeed. Capable of being every bit as ruthless as his hostess when occasion demanded, he extricated himself from the clinging hold and put his arm protectively round Melly.

'*Bonsoir, Fabienne,*' Charles greeted politely as he closed the door behind them. '*Ça va?*'

With a little shrug, she answered, '*Ça va,*' before leading the way into the lounge. They were obviously the last to arrive, and Melly smiled vaguely round at the four couples present, all of whom she had met previously, before going with Charles to shake their hands. It always amused Melly the way everyone always shook hands, even if they'd only seen each other a short while previously, because, considering the origins of the custom, that you shook hands in order to prove you weren't concealing a dagger, it would seem that the French had been more dagger-orientated than any other race. Except perhaps for the Italians.

'Why the little secret smile?' David asked softly as he walked beside her into the dining-room. 'And may I add how positively blooming you look?'

'You may, thank you.'

'So now tell me why you were smiling,' he repeated as he held her chair out for her and seated himself beside her.

'Oh, just thoughts. About knives,' she tacked on mischievously.

'Knives in general, or particular?' he queried humorously. 'Marking down future victims, Melly? Now who will be your first, I wonder? My esteemed wife?' Watching her carefully for her reaction, he was satisfied when she looked startled. 'Think I don't know how she feels about your husband? Think I don't see and hear? I do, Melly.

I see and hear a great many things people might hope I don't.'

Wondering if that was an oblique dig at herself and Charles, she asked softly, 'Such as?'

'Such as, Charles couldn't give a damn about Fabienne. Which means, neither need you. She is afraid,' he said gently. 'Be charitable, hm? You can afford to be, you know.'

'Why is she afraid?' she asked equally gently.

'Because she is frightened of growing old. Time is passing for her, and, no matter how many times I tell her that women in their forties are more attractive than those in their twenties, she disbelieves me. It is sad, no?'

'Yes,' she agreed. Feeling obscurely guilty for the way she had treated his wife in the past, writing her off as a fool, she apologised quietly, 'I'm sorry.'

'I know. You are a nice person, Melly. Far too nice for this crowd.' With his gentle smile, he turned away as the lady on his other side asked him a question.

Charles was seated on her left, Fabienne beside him, and as the soup was placed before them she was content to apply herself to the meal and listen to the buzz of conversation round the table. Probably the same conversation as always, she thought with an inward smile. Take away the couture dresses, the expensive jewels, and they could have been any social gathering anywhere. From any walk of life. She could vividly remember her mother saying, after one of her bridge evenings, 'The same conversations, Melly! The same boring people!' People were people, whatever walk of life they came from; whatever class of society;

just the speech and the clothes were different. Life only became interesting when you met with different people, held different conversations. Unless you were with Charles, of course, she thought with an inward smile of satisfaction.

Still hoarding the memory of his kiss, she smiled her thanks at the waiter as he removed her plate and replaced it with another one. Charles was talking to the man opposite him, Sebastien, and totally ignoring Fabienne, and for once Melly felt quite sorry for her. David was still talking to his other neighbour, so she was free to listen in to the babble of talk being conducted in a mixture of French and English. She became quite intrigued by the soft snatches she could hear, especially the bit about the house, and Jean-Marc, not being won in a poker game. She couldn't hear all they said, because, with Charles and herself being at the other end of the table, they spoke, of necessity, very softly, but she did understand that it was a tale put about by her husband in order to keep people guessing. Or throw dust in their eyes. Why, she had no idea. Nor, apparently, did they. She could understand why he hadn't told *them* the truth, but why not her? Odd. Did he want her to think he was more of a gambler than he was? Did he not want her to know that he could afford more things than he said? She knew he couldn't be poor, otherwise he wouldn't be able to follow the lifestyle he did. And he'd been more than generous over her own wardrobe, and giving her money to spend...

'You're looking very serious,' an amused feminine voice said from across the table, and she looked up with a blink at Sebastien's wife.

'Oh, sorry, Victoire, I was miles away.' She liked Victoire and her husband, two of the few people she did like in this set. They were both about ten years older than Melly, and unbelievably kind.

With a quick look either side to make sure no one was listening, she asked softly, 'How did the scan go today?'

'Oh, fine,' she said automatically. 'I have to go back next week for another.'

A look of amusement crossing her face, she said portentously, 'Dr Lafage!'

'Why, yes; do you know him?'

'But of course. He was my doctor also. Did he say the baby was small?'

'Yes!'

'And you have been worrying? Do not. He tells me my baby is small! And then I have two! So you must not be worrying!'

A great deal relieved, because she had been worrying, she smiled gratefully at the other woman, refused the sweet she was offered by the waiter, then turned at the pressure on her thigh from her husband.

'All right?' he asked gently. 'You've been very quiet.'

'I'm always very quiet,' she teased.

'Not always,' he argued, with gentle reference to their earlier conversation. Giving her a very nice smile that affected her as it always did, made her feel warm, and special, he continued, 'However, I think I will take you home. You look a little tired. It has been a long, worrying day for you. So home. And bed.'

With him? she wondered with a tingle of excitement. With no desire to argue, she smiled her thanks to Fabienne and David, waved goodbye to the others, and, collecting her wrap, accompanied Charles out to the car.

'It was not so bad, hm?' he queried lightly as he drove them the few miles home to their house.

'No, not so bad.' I heard something odd, which I didn't understand, she wanted to add, but it wasn't so bad. 'Are you going on to the casino?'

'No, I've changed my mind.' Directing a roguish smile in her direction that set her heart beating unevenly, he pulled into the drive.

Jean-Marc had left the lights on for them, and, unusually, was waiting up.

'Getting fussy in your old age, Jean-Marc?' Charles teased. 'You don't usually wait up when you know I'm with *madame*.'

'*Non*,' he agreed gravely, 'but I could hardly go to my bed and leave the visitor alone.'

'Visitor?' they said together.

'*Mais oui*. A friend for *madame*. She has been waiting some hours. I took it upon myself to make her up a bed in the spare room.' Turning, he led the way along the hall and quietly opened the lounge door. '*Voilà. Mademoiselle Pritchard*.'

Caught off balance, Melly stared in disbelief. Ah, no, she mentally denied. Please no, not now, not when things were going so well. That's not fair! Not Anita, the one person who knew of her fantasy. Knew of the real reason she had come to Deauville, and who was, as Melly knew only too well, quite incapable of keeping quiet. Anita could, and probably did, talk the hind leg off a donkey. At school she had been known as Old Verbosity. What she didn't know, she would make up. What she did know, she would embroider. All Melly had to do now was stop her, before she opened her mouth. Which would be a bit like trying to stop the ice cap melting under the desert sun.

She never meant to be malicious. Never meant to get people into trouble, but it was a sad fact of life that Nita could never keep her thoughts to herself. The only hope she might have was if Charles was struck by instant deafness; or Nita struck dumb. Only in real life such conveniences never happened. And Charles was never going to understand. She knew he wasn't.

CHAPTER FOUR

'MELLY!' Arms wide, Nita advanced on her friend. The only friend she had, in actual fact. 'You look terrific!'

'Tha——'

'So elegant, so—chic! Wow! That dress must have cost an absolute fortune! No wonder you pursued him so relentlessly,' she laughed. 'So would I if he could buy me those sort of clothes! And oh, Mel, it is good to see you!'

'You too,' Melly said with quiet exasperation. Only Nita could give away so much in so short a time. With a faint smile, she bent to kiss her friend on the cheek. Intending to whisper to her not to say anything else, anything at all, until they could talk, she didn't get the chance. After one quick hug Nita released herself and advanced on Charles.

Her head on one side, she stood in front of him, her homely face so full of pleasure that it would have taken a very hard heart not to be affected by it. 'So you're Charles! Well, I can quite see now why Melly should be so besotted!' Thrusting out her hand to be shaken, she laughed delightedly when Charles grasped her shoulders and bent to kiss her on each cheek.

'Hello, Nita,' he greeted solemnly. 'It is a pleasure to meet you at long last.'

'Melly's told you about me?' she asked, surprised.

'But of course. You are her friend...'

'Well, yes, but, well, to be honest, people usually keep very quiet about me!'

'Surely not?' he denied, his face still solemn, but his eyes alight with amusement.

'Oh, they do!' she insisted. 'They also avoid me in the street! But Melly and I have been friends for ages! Haven't we?' she swung round to demand.

'Ye——'

'And we tell each other everything! I'm so glad it all worked out. I mean, you could have been furious! I——'

'Nita!' Melly broke in desperately, then laughed when the other two looked at her in surprise. 'Lovely as it is to see you,' she carried on lamely, 'it is very late. Would you mind very much if we talked in the morning?'

'Oh, gosh, sorry, Mel. I keep forgetting you're pregnant. I expect you're tired.'

'But not you?' Charles queried humorously.

'Heavens, no! I'm never tired. Probably I don't need much sleep. Some people don't, you know. My mother always despaired when I wouldn't go to bed. Even as a child——'

'Nita,' Melly broke in. 'Sit!'

With a little giggle, Nita sat.

'Now,' Melly continued, half amused, half horrified by the thought of what further revelations Nita might manage to come out with before she could divert her, 'have you eaten?'

'Oh, yes. The delightful Jean-Marc made me something. Where on earth did you find him?' she demanded. 'He's priceless! Just like out of a book, and why didn't you tell me——?'

'Nita! Would you like a drink? Coffee, tea, whisky...'

'Martini?' she asked hopefully.

With a chuckle, Charles walked across to the bar. 'Mixed? Or as it comes?'

'Oh, can I have a mixed one? Shaken, not stirred?' she asked, with such hopeful enthusiasm that both Melly and Charles laughed.

'Certainly you may, and, while I'm mixing it, tell me why I might have been furious.'

'Her turning up unexpectedly,' Melly put in quickly. 'I expect that's what she meant. Wasn't it, Nita?' she added meaningfully. She might just as well have saved her breath.

'No, of course not, silly, I knew you wouldn't mind me coming to see you. No, I meant your pursuit of Charles.'

'Pursuit!' Melly scoffed. 'Stop romanticising...'

'I'm not! There's no need to be embarrassed; I'm sure Charles doesn't mind. Do you?' she queried, turning to him.

'Not in the least,' he said blandly. 'Explain.'

'Oh, you,' she laughed teasingly, 'I expect you know it all backwards and forwards about Melly pretending she came out to see her grandfather's grave, but really coming to find you. I bet you had a good laugh about it! I think it's really romantic. I mean, fancy loving someone since you were ten years old—and then actually getting to marry them!'

'Ten?' Charles queried lightly.

'Well, yes, I think so; it was ten, wasn't it, Melly?'

As she leant back in her chair a feeling of fatalism stole over her. She had known that one day he would find out. People always did, eventually, so in a way she supposed she had been expecting it. Not so soon perhaps, but one day. Fairy stories didn't always have a happy ending. Knowing there was very little she could do, or say, that would give Nita's words an innocence they clearly didn't have, she accepted the inevitable with a sick feeling in her stomach. Protestations now would only make things worse. It was no good fervently wishing it was a nightmare she could now wake up from; she would just have to hope that Charles would understand. Or at least take Nita's words with a pinch of salt. Taking a determined little breath, she tried to minimise the damage. 'A childhood fantasy,' she explained lightly. 'Knight in shining armour and all that. You know what ten-year-old girls are like.'

'No, tell me.'

Staring at him, never having heard quite that tone in his voice before, she retorted awkwardly, 'There's nothing to tell. Nita's just teasing you.'

'Are you?' he asked her quietly.

Staring from one to the other, Nita suddenly flushed. 'I did it again, didn't I?' Which was about the worst thing she could have said, and, if it had been anyone else but Nita, Melly would have known they were being vindictive, malicious. But it wasn't anyone else, and Nita was just, well, not very bright sometimes. You could hit her over the head with a nuance, and she still wouldn't see it.

'You didn't do anything,' Charles denied smoothly as he handed her her drink. 'Melly's had a long day, and she's tired. Aren't you, darling?'

'Yes,' she agreed quietly.

'So why not go on up to bed? I'm sure Nita won't mind, will you?'

'Goodness, no.'

'There,' Charles continued silkily, 'you go on up, and I will entertain Nita for a while.'

Which was exactly what Melly was afraid of. But protesting, or insisting she stay, wouldn't affect the outcome, she knew that. If Charles was determined to talk to Nita alone then talk to her he would. Holding his eyes, she read the message quite plainly: go to bed. Nita and I will talk. And find out everything there is to know about you since the age of ten. She didn't even have the comfort of knowing that Nita would now keep quiet. Having put her foot in it, she would try to justify everything, emphasise how much Melly loved him. She would think she was helping. Miserable and upset at hurting her friend, she would unwittingly proceed to make bad worse.

'I'm sorry,' Nita whispered as she kissed Melly goodnight. 'Why on earth didn't you tell me he didn't know? I mean, it just never occurred to me! But he must love you, I mean, you having a baby and everything.'

'Yes, don't worry about it. I'll see you in the morning. Goodnight.' Nita had obviously never heard of casual sex, or, if she had, would be convinced that it was something neither herself nor her friend Melly would ever indulge in. Not that it had been casual, but, to the romantic Nita, if you had sex it was because you were violently in love with each other. No other reason would ever have occurred to her.

Feeling cold, and empty, and tired, she slipped from the room and went slowly upstairs. Charles *might* be amused, she thought without much conviction; and, even if he wasn't, surely he would see that their meeting by the harbour had been accidental? And certainly he would know that she hadn't planned seduction; that she had merely been offering comfort after Laurent's death. And if she could minimise the obsession, make him see that Nita was given to exaggeration... With a long sigh she went to stand at the window. There was no point in speculating. Charles would think what Charles would think, and all she could do was try to explain; try to make him understand. No point either, in going to bed, or not yet, anyway. After talking to Nita Charles would want to hear her side of the story. Nothing if not fair was Charles.

It wasn't very long before she heard them both come up. Heard Charles wish Nita a pleasant goodnight; heard her bedroom door close. Taking a deep, steadying breath, she turned to face the door as it slowly opened.

Carefully closing the door behind him, he walked to stand in front of her. Observing her silently for a few moments, his eyes steady, expressionless, he finally said, 'It would seem, wouldn't it, that I have been taken for even more of a fool than I thought I was?'

'More of...' She frowned, not understanding.

'But of course. I knew—no, let us be pedantic about this, shall we? I suspected that your visit to Deauville was not entirely to visit your grandfather's grave. I suspected that life at home had become perhaps more intolerable than usual. I suspected that I was to be used as an escape route. Not permanently,' he continued in the same smooth, hateful voice, 'certainly not that. But as a temporary haven, perhaps. I could even understand, forgive, because I was fond of you.'

'No! It had nothing to do with home!'

'Did it not? Then we must assume, mustn't we, that Anita's reading of the situation was the correct one?'

'No.' Hating this so much, hating the note of distaste in his voice, she whispered painfully, 'And if you thought I had come to see you, why——?'

'Why did I never say? Because I liked you, felt sorry for you, because I, of all people, knew what your home life was like. I assumed it was embarrassment that prevented you from confiding in me. I respected that, and went along with the fiction.'

Feeling helpless, and trapped, she stared at him, almost mesmerised. Had she ever really known him at all? Gone was the humour, the charm; now she saw him as presumably his business associates might see him. Tough, in control, hard. This was the Charles who had made a success of his life. The Charles who saw clearly, whose judgement was rarely at fault.

'No? It isn't true?'

'No. Yes,' she agreed defeatedly, 'in a way. I——'

'Yes or no, Melly?'

Slumping tiredly, she searched his face for a trace of compassion, and found none. It was carefully devoid of expression. Neither hard nor soft. Not angry, not understanding. Only able to guess at what Nita had told him, she qualified, 'Based on exaggeration, elaboration, a bending of the truth, but basically, yes, it's true.'

'You deliberately set out to trap me?' he asked in the same awful, quiet voice.

If he had sounded cold, or condemning, it might have been easier, they could have had a flaming great row about it, cleared the air, but it wasn't, was merely conversational. As always. Charles never lost his temper, or if he did she had never seen him. 'No,' she denied, 'not deliberate, not a trap. That was never my intention.'

'But you did know I was here?'

'Yes.'

'And visiting your grandfather's grave was just a hook to hang the visit on?'

'Not entirely...' With a quiet little sigh she shook her head. Only the truth would do, anything else would be even more degrading. 'Yes, visiting his grave was just an excuse.'

'I see. All these years,' he commented softly, 'stalking me——'

'No, Charles,' she protested desperately. 'No, it wasn't I——'

'No?' he queried. 'What would you call it?'

Biting her lip, she turned away and stared through the window while she considered how to explain. 'A need to be near you,' she murmured, 'to be able to see you, even if only from a distance. It's like, well, like a junkie needing a fix, I suppose. An alcoholic needing a drink. I don't know why I had this obsession. It was shaming, degrading, and yet I was unable to help myself.' Turning to watch him, needing to see his expression, she continued, 'I've never asked anything of you, deliberately so. Never expected anything. I just seem to have this over-whelming need to be near you. I would never de-liberately hurt you, embarrass you—or compromise you in any way.'

'Then why the pretence? Why not be honest from the beginning? Why, when you parked at the harbour that first day here, and you saw me on the yacht—because you did see me, didn't you?'

'Yes,' she admitted.

'Then why pretend you didn't? Why walk away, knowing I would follow? Call out? Exclaim? "What a surprise, Melly, how lovely to see you..." Even then, when we went for coffee, you could have told me.'

'How? What would I say?' she asked miserably. 'I came out because I couldn't stay away? That I needed a sight of you? You'd have thought I'd run mad.'

'Then why not come up to me on the yacht? All you had to say was, "Hi, I knew you were in Deauville and, while looking up Grandfather's grave, I thought I'd come and say hello." That would have been normal. I'd have been pleased to see you, taken you out, but without the pretence. There's every possibility that events would have followed the same course, but without the sham.'

'I know all that!' she exclaimed helplessly. 'You think I don't? I can't even explain my behaviour to myself, so how could I ever explain it to you? I know that's what I should have done! What any normal person would have done! But I couldn't!'

'But why?' he asked in genuine puzzlement.

'I don't know why, damn you! If I did I could maybe do something about it! In every other area of my life I'm a rational, if not to say predictable human being! I can be objective, intelligent—but with you, Charles, I just don't know! Since the first day I saw you, when I was ten, when you rescued me from those bullies trying to push me into the pond, you've lived in my heart, my mind, my whole being, and I can't get you out! You think I haven't tried?' she asked despairingly. 'You think I don't know what a fool I am?'

There was a short, painful silence, while he presumably thought about her words, and then he asked quietly, 'Who else knows?'

'No one,' she denied wearily.

'Not your parents?'

'No.'

'Then why confide in Nita? I should have thought she was the last person to share confidences with! Good God, Melly, her tongue runs on wheels!'

'I know, but oh, it's difficult to explain. We were at school together, she had no other friends, and because I was nice to her, I suppose, she latched on to me. She seemed to think she owed me something, needed to defend me at every opportunity, and when those same boys, who were also at my school, taunted me about the great hero rescuing me from the pond Nita was there, and, Nita being Nita, she joined in my defence of you. I pointed you out to her one day and every time there was gossip about you, an article in the paper—because you have to admit you were rather notorious, Charles,' she added in an effort to lighten the atmosphere, 'she would carefully save it to show me. And over the years she continued to do so. I think I'd confessed once, in a moment of weakness, how I felt about you, probably round about the age of fifteen, and Nita kept it up. Most of what she said to you was probably fantasising, because when I grew up I never discussed you with anyone, including Nita, but because she was my friend, and probably because she thought it was something she could do for me, even if only in a jokey way, she would keep me up to date with any information she came across about you. She never knew, still doesn't, how I really felt, how obsessed I was...'

'But it was she who told you I was in Deauville? She who showed you the picture of *Wanderer*?'

'Yes. But I didn't tell her I was coming here...'

'No, apparently your mother did. Nita put two and two together—and when she heard of our marriage, and about the baby...'

'She thought the fairy-tale had a happy ending. And all due to her,' Melly concluded sadly.

Staring back through the window, watching the lights in the town, she wondered a trifle bleakly whether anyone else was ever blessed, or cursed, with such a friend. When he made no comment she turned to look at him. His face looked carved, bleak, and distaste still twisted his mouth. 'You don't believe me, do you?'

'No,' he said flatly. 'If I didn't know you? Then yes, maybe. But I *do* know you, thought I knew everything there was to know about you. And you even admitted yourself that you were stuck in Beckford, told me how your parents didn't want you to leave. That you felt trapped, stifled, and through no fault of your own were left to bear the brunt of your brother's death. Smothered with affection, hedged in by restrictions because they were afraid they would lose you too, I offered a chance of escape. If you married you would have to leave. But who in Beckford was there to marry? No one. You didn't travel, work away, in London or another big town, so what chance was there to meet anyone? But there was someone you knew. Someone wealthy, with a lifestyle you could only dream about, and Nita herself mentioned how you had always wanted to travel, be able to afford to dress properly——'

'But that was said in fun!' she protested. Damn Nita and her big mouth!

'Was it?'

'Yes!' she insisted.

'Yet, if I recall, her exact words were, "No wonder you pursued him so relentlessly."'

'As a joke! A silly schoolgirl joke!' she persisted desperately. 'Oh, come on, Charles, you know what girls are like! It was probably said when I was fourteen! One day I'm going to marry a wealthy man. Rich and handsome and famous—you know the sort of thing.'

'Yes, I do,' he agreed smoothly. 'And in my experience those same fourteen-year-olds grow up to do exactly that. Or try to.'

'Then you must have had some lousy experiences,' she retorted.

'I have.'

Looking at him sharply, seeing no humour on his face, only a bleak certainty that he was right, she asked quietly, 'Have you?'

'Oh, yes.'

'And you now think I'm one of them?'

Regarding her steadily, he nodded. 'Yes, Melly, I'm rather afraid I do. You see, I also know about your father's financial difficulties——'

'But that was years ago!' she exclaimed, horrified, as she began to see which way his mind was working.

'True—and are you now telling me that they have been resolved? That you don't have to assist them financially? Well?'

'Boy,' she retorted bitterly, 'Nita has been busy, hasn't she? All right,' she admitted harshly, 'yes, I help them out financially, but it has nothing to do with why I came here!'

He didn't need to answer; his sceptical expression did it for him. Staring at her, he gave a twisted smile. 'Obsession,' he said softly. 'How ironic. I left my home and family to escape obsession, and ended up by marrying it. One should perhaps be amused by the incongruity. Only I don't feel very amused right at this moment.'

Not altogether understanding what he meant, and with an ache in her heart that was too deep ever to give voice to, she looked down. A calculated plan, that's what he thought. And it wasn't, not really. 'Oh, Charles!' she exclaimed sadly. Laying her hand on his arm, she winced when he pointedly moved so that her hand dropped limply to her side. She felt sick and empty and suddenly too exhausted to explain further, even if there had been any point, which she didn't think there was. He was obviously in no mood to listen. Perhaps later, when he had thought it over. It might even be best to go away for a while... 'Do you want me to leave?' she asked quietly. When he didn't answer, only continued to regard her, his face empty, she gave a jerky sigh. Her voice a thin, husky thread of sound, she added shakily, 'I'll get packed up in the morning. Go back to Beckford. Naturally I'll let you know when the baby's born.'

'Naturally,' he repeated without inflexion. 'No tears, Melly? No remonstrations? Protestations of innocence?'

'No,' she denied emptily. 'I'll just go away. No fuss, no drama.' A few simple words, and he would never know how much it hurt her to say them.

'And how much will it cost me?' he asked cynically. 'For there to be no fuss, no drama?'

Looking up at him, her hurt and shock reflected in her eyes, she whispered, 'Nothing, Charles. It will cost you nothing. I told you, I never wanted to hurt you, never wanted to cause you pain. The same goes for financial loss. Why should you pay for being cheated? Because that's what you feel, isn't it? Cheated? I never meant to do that,' she added, almost to herself. 'Never meant to cheat, just take a few crumbs and hope they would be enough. Only of course crumbs never are. You take a chance on life; if you win, great, if you don't, tough. Don't whine, don't grumble. You should understand that—you take chances all the time.'

'Not with people, Melly. Not ever with people.'

'No,' she agreed unhappily. That was true; he only ever risked himself. Thinking about it, about the way he was, about what she had done, what she had maybe robbed him of, she continued in the same quiet, emotionless voice, 'I knew you never loved me. Probably would never love me, but we had friendship, and I think I hoped that would be enough. Hoped that I could make you happy. Not ecstatic,' she added with a funny little smile, 'not fulfilled, perhaps, but content.'

'Rather arrogant of you.'

With a flush of anguish and mortification, she looked down. 'Yes, I suppose it was.' Yet he had admitted earlier, before Nita had come, that he had been happy with her.

'And the pregnancy?' he persisted. 'That was planned?'

'No!' she protested, shocked that he could even consider it.

'Really?' he queried again, with that hateful trace of sarcasm.

'Yes, really! My God, do you honestly think me so irresponsible as to bring a new life into the world with no guarantee of its future? Of course it wasn't planned!'

'Yet you forgot to mention that you weren't taking precautions——'

'I didn't forget to mention! I never even gave it a thought! You were hurt, aching, and I was there. It wasn't planned—it just happened! Whatever else you might think of me,' she added earnestly, 'please don't ever think that!'

'Well, certainly I couldn't accuse you of engineering Laurent's accident——'

'Well, of course I couldn't!'

'But you were very swiftly on hand to offer comfort. You were very quick to see an opportunity and grasp it.'

'No!' But she had, she thought miserably. Had deliberately stayed when she knew she should have gone. But, feeling as she had, how could she have

gone? 'Oh, Charles!' she exclaimed sadly. 'You
have no idea, have you, how it feels to love someone
so much, and with such intensity, that to be forced
to witness their pain, their hurt, and not be able to
do anything to help crucifies you? It isn't something you can calculate, take advantage of; it's like
the nose on your face: just there. And if you love
like that nothing on earth would ever make you
hurt them, deliberately cause them pain. I had no
thoughts of intimacy, marriage, when I came out.
I just needed to see you. See that you were all right,
be near you, just for a moment. The rest, well, it
just happened,' she concluded lamely. But he would
never understand feelings like that. He couldn't.
And yet, hadn't he felt those emotions when
Laurent had died? And what had he meant about
leaving home because of an obsession?

Swaying with tiredness, she leaned against the
wall and watched him. So dear, so loved. So
blinkered. She should never have married him, of
course; never have agreed to his proposal; but the
temptation had been too great. And why had he
proposed? If he had been suspicious of her mo-
tives... 'Why did you ask me to marry you?' she
asked quietly. 'If you thought I deliberately sought
you out...'

'Because of the baby. Because it was my responsibility, and because I liked you, thought I
understood you. I would never otherwise have done
so.'

No, of course he wouldn't. He could have had
anyone he chose. 'I'll leave in the morning,' she
repeated listlessly.

Still staring at her, examining her wan face, he shook his head. 'No,' he denied coldly. 'Your hospital notes are here; you know the doctors, nurses, you're booked in—no. You will stay here until the baby is born.'

How? she wondered. How could she stay here, knowing that he despised her? It wasn't just a few days, it was weeks! She could not spend weeks watching him grow colder.

'No,' she whispered, 'I——'

'It's not open for discussion, Melly,' he said flatly. 'You will stay until after the baby is born.'

And then? Go back to Beckford? With or without the baby? she wanted to ask, only dared not. If it was something he hadn't yet considered she didn't want to put the idea into his head. But even though she would not, had no right to fight for his love, his understanding, she had every right to fight for her child, and would do so, if it proved necessary. The possible loss of her child would not be accepted with the fatalism with which she accepted the loss of Charles. It would not be accepted at all.

'And you will say nothing of this to anyone. Anyone,' he repeated. 'You owe me that, I think, don't you?'

'Yes, Charles, I owe you that,' she agreed in the same quiet voice she had used all along.

'Very well, you will continue to behave as though nothing has happened. You will make Nita's visit a pleasant one; reassure her; behave to my friends as you have always behaved, and neither by hint, nor deed, will you let anyone know the truth.'

And what is the truth, Charles? That you believe yourself to have been ill-used? Or that you can't accept that someone might be vulnerable, have an obsession? And why did he not want to cut his losses now? Why not make a clean break? Because he wanted to see the baby born?

'Well?'

Nodding tiredly, she watched him turn and walk away. And only when the bedroom door closed behind him did she allow herself to cry. She had no rights over him, he had no feelings on which she could tug, she had known that, had known that this day would come. Why had she never known how much it would hurt? Blinded by tears, she blundered towards the bathroom and began preparing for bed.

CHAPTER FIVE

'BEHAVE as normal,' Charles had said. Sure. With a hollow laugh, her eyes still puffy from her tears, Melly walked along the landing. She had barely slept all night, and she felt like death. Taking a deep breath, and pinning a smile on her face, she tapped on Nita's door and went in. Her friend was sitting in the chair beside the bed, fully dressed, hands folded primly in her lap.

'I was afraid to come down,' she confessed sheepishly. 'I've been sitting here for hours!'

'Hours?' Melly queried disbelievingly. It was barely nine o'clock, but Nita looked so woebegone that Melly was unable to repress a smile. She wanted to hate her, blame her, but she couldn't. 'Fool,' she said fondly.

'I know,' she agreed with a long sigh. 'I'm so sorry, Mel.' Giving her friend a searching glance, she exclaimed unhappily, 'You've been crying!'

Knowing how pointless it was to deny it, she gave a crooked smile. 'It's the pregnancy, it makes me weepy.' Holding Nita's eyes, she silently begged her to believe it.

'Nothing to do with Charles?'

'No, of course not. What did you think he's been doing? Beating me?'

'No! But—well, how do you tell if he's angry?' she burst out.

'You don't,' Melly said quietly, 'he doesn't let it show.'

'Never?' Nita asked in disbelief.

'No.' Not to her knowledge, anyway, and to be angry you had to care, passionately, and Charles didn't, or not about her. He cared about other things, his various businesses, his horses, and presumably, in those things, he was different again. You didn't amass huge wealth by being kind and gentle, at least she supposed you didn't, but until now she had only ever seen the nice side of him. She had seen him anguished, over Laurent's death; and she knew, or suspected, that he had been hurt by something that had happened in his childhood; but she had never seen him lose his temper. Perhaps that was reserved for larger issues. Neither had she seen him cold, and ruthless. Until yesterday. With an inward sigh she forced herself to sound normal. 'Come on, come down and have some breakfast; then we'll decide what we want to do.'

For the first time since their marriage there was no Charles to hold out her chair. No Charles to pour her coffee. Jean-Marc performed that little courtesy, with aplomb, with careful neutrality. '*M'sieu* had to go out, *madame*,' he informed her, 'but asked me to tell you that he will be back this evening in time to take you both to the casino. He thought that Mademoiselle Pritchard would enjoy it.'

'Yes, thank you, Jean-Marc,' Melly said quietly. 'I'm sure she will.'

'Will there be anything further?'

'No, I expect we will be out for most of the day.'

'Then I will attend to my duties.' With a little dip of the head for both ladies, he retreated and closed the door quietly behind him.

The whole performance was rather spoilt by Nita's giggle. 'Oh, Melly, he's priceless! Does he always talk to you like that?'

With a faint smile she nodded. 'Usually. Sometimes he speaks in French, to test me. Sometimes in English, to confuse me. So, where would you like to go today? A look at the shops in Deauville? Honfleur? Caen?'

With a hesitant air, as though not wishing to be a nuisance, she asked tentatively, 'Is Bayeux very far away?'

'Bayeux? Why, no, about an hour's drive. Maybe a little more. Why? Did you want to see the tapestry?'

Nodding, she exclaimed, 'I've always wanted to see it! Ever since we learned about it in school! Is it too far? I mean, you might not feel like traipsing round——'

'I'm only pregnant, Nita! Not an invalid! Of course it isn't too far!' Staring thoughtfully at her friend for a few minutes, forcing her own troubles to the back of her mind, she gave a little nod. 'Right. What we'll do is take the coast road. I can show you the landing beaches. Juno, Sword, et cetera, and you have to see the memorial on the cliff-top at Pointe du Hoc, where Lieutenant Colonel James Rudder, and what was left of his Rangers, scaled the one-hundred-foot cliffs on D-Day to seize the fortified enemy positions which controlled the landing approaches to Omaha and Utah beaches.'

With an infectious laugh, Nita teased, 'Shades of John Wayne?'

'Mm, a bit, but mostly you just feel an overwhelming sadness for all the brave men who died. The bunkers are still there,' she added sombrely, 'the gun emplacements, with guns—pretty much as it was left after the war, I imagine.'

'And you can walk all across it?' Nita asked in surprise.

'Yes. I must admit, it surprised me too. In England it would have been fenced off, the guns removed to a place of safety. There would have been graffiti on the walls—and yet here,' she added almost to herself, 'was only respect.' Shaking off her sombre mood, she continued more lightly, 'We can have a quick look in the war museums if you'd like—they really are worth a visit. The American cemetery... I know a nice little place for lunch... Then Bayeux, and you really must see the cathedral...'

'But if we're going out this evening,' Nita protested, 'won't it be too much for you?'

'Heavens, no!' Melly exclaimed, perhaps too forcefully. And if I keep busy, don't leave myself time to think, I'll be fine. Her misery over the split with Charles, especially after the tender way he had behaved to her the day before, before Nita had arrived to spoil it all, overshadowed her fears for the baby, and made her forget her need to rest.

During that long tiring day she told herself repeatedly that hearts didn't really break, they only got a little bruised, a bit battered; but it felt broken, no matter what was said. And taking Nita to all the places that Charles had once taken her to proved a severe test of her resolve to behave normally, pretend. Everywhere they walked, everywhere they stood reminded her of another day, a day of warmth and laughter, of sadness, emotion and togetherness. A day when they had been the very best of friends.

'It brings a lump to your throat, doesn't it?' Nita said quietly as they stared at the row upon row of white crosses in the American cemetery.

Feeling pretty choked herself, Melly merely nodded. So many deaths, thousand upon thousand; it made her problems seem pretty insignificant. Petty. 'Come on, let's go and get some lunch.'

They returned to Deauville well after seven to find Charles sitting in the lounge, reading. At their entrance he put aside his paper and got politely to his feet. 'Hi,' he said with a smile for Nita, and if it didn't quite reach his steady grey eyes only Melly noticed. 'Have a good day?'

'Magnificent!' Nita exclaimed. 'We went to the landing beaches, and then Bayeux. So much history! And the tapestry! Have you seen it?' she asked him.

After a small hesitation, and a sharp look at Melly, he admitted, 'Yes, it surprised me too. I'd always imagined it as carpet-sized, not long and narrow and winding all round that passageway.'

'Yes. So much work. Amazing.'

'And now you're both thoroughly worn out.'

'Well, I certainly am!' Nita exclaimed. 'So goodness knows how Melly feels!' Collapsing on to the sofa, she kicked off her shoes.

'No, goodness knows how Melly feels,' he repeated quietly, and she felt a shiver of apprehension. With a smile, that to Melly looked extremely false, he asked Nita, 'Too tired to go out tonight?'

'No!' she denied with a laugh. 'Just give me a drink, let me have half an hour to relax, and then I'll be fighting fit again!'

'Good.' As he turned to his wife his tone altered slightly, became cooler. 'Melly? I think you had better stay here and rest. You know what the doctor said. You don't want to jeopardise the health of the baby,' he added pointedly. 'Or your own,' he murmured, a little too late to be entirely convincing.

'No,' she agreed. 'Although I didn't do too much walking. Mostly I sat in the car.' Avoiding his eyes, she continued, 'But I will, I think, go and lie down for a while. What time did you want to leave? About nine?'

'Yes. I'll take Nita for a meal, and then I thought she might like to watch the cabaret before going on to the casino.'

'Sounds fine. I'll see you both later.' With a vague smile, aimed at neither of them, she went up to her room and lay on the bed. Fighting back tears, she took deliberate deep breaths in an attempt to release the pain in her chest. So that told you, Melly. You aren't wanted.

A few minutes later the door quietly opened, and closed.

'How dare you jeopardise the health of the baby?' he gritted savagely as he advanced across the room. 'Rest, the doctor said!'

'I did——'

'You did not! Jean-Marc says you have been out since ten this morning! You think to punish me?'

'No! And I did rest! I stayed in the car——' The hesitant tap at the door made her break off.

His mouth tight, Charles walked across to open it. Giving her a warning look, he pulled it wide, and Melly hastily composed herself before Nita advanced into the room.

'Oh, is it all right?' she asked awkwardly.

'Yes, of course,' Charles said smoothly. 'I was just going; I'll leave you two to gossip.'

'Sorry, I didn't mean to interrupt anything,' she apologised to Melly as the door closed behind him.

'You didn't.' Hoisting herself up on the pillows, she waited.

Advancing on the bed, her face troubled, Nita said quietly, 'It isn't all right, is it?'

'Yes, of course it is,' she lied as convincingly as she knew how. 'He's just a bit upset because he thought I'd been walking round the landing beaches—which, of course, I hadn't. Don't worry about it.'

'Honest? I couldn't bear to think that I was the cause of you having another row.'

'We didn't have any rows. Now go away and rest or you won't be fit to go out tonight.'

Still looking troubled, she trailed out, and Melly heard her go back downstairs. Going to speak to Charles about it? she wondered. Knowing Nita, yes, that was precisely what she would do. And make things even worse? Yes, she had a positive evil genius for that. Oh, Nita. A friend in need was a friend indeed. What idiot said that? Whoever it was, he obviously hadn't met Nita.

She could faintly hear her voice, and Charles in reply, but not the words—and when all was said and done, she thought tiredly, she only had herself to blame. Hers had been the fantasy, the hope.

Her eyes filling with tears, she rolled on to her side and clutched the pillow to her face in order to stifle her sobs.

'Melly?'

Waking with a start, she stared up at Charles as he stood beside the bed. He'd switched on the bedside lamp, and with the light behind him it was difficult to see his expression; although perhaps that was just as well. He was dressed in his dinner jacket, and, for the first time that she could remember, he looked alien. Unobtainable. How long had he been standing watching her sleep? she wondered. A few minutes? Thinking what?

'It's almost eight-thirty,' he informed her quietly, and without inflexion. 'Nita and I are just off.'

Wanting nothing more than to close her eyes again and go back to sleep, pretend that all was right with her world, pride dictated otherwise. 'Oh, right,' she whispered lamely, and if her voice was a little husky he would no doubt put that down to her being only half awake. Feeling far too vulnerable lying down, and quite unaware of the unhappiness showing in her lovely eyes, she rolled into a sitting position. 'It's kind of you to take her...'

'Yes,' he agreed flatly. 'Jean-Marc will bring you up a tray in a few minutes. There will be no need for you to wait up.' Without waiting for her answer, he left.

He'd sounded so cold, so emotionless. So *hurt*. Her face bleak, she leaned tiredly back against the pillows just as Nita put her head round the door. God, it was like Piccadilly Circus.

'How do you feel?' she asked quietly, almost as though talking to an invalid.

'I'm fine. All ready?'

'Yes.' Coming further into the room, she asked hesitantly, 'Do I look all right? I wasn't sure how I was supposed to dress for the casino. And with Charles looking so elegant...'

'You look fine,' Melly reassured. 'The classic little black dress is always acceptable.' Her head on one side, she added, 'Why not borrow my pearls? They'll sit just nicely in that neckline.'

'Oh, may I?' As she walked across to the jewellery box on the dressing-table she suddenly halted and looked dubious. 'Are they very expensive?'

'No,' Melly lied. Charles had bought them for her, and he would never buy rubbish. But they had been bought to wear, not sit in their box. Even if he didn't love her, he would still buy the best. 'Take the earrings as well,' she insisted, and when Nita had put them on she smiled approvingly. 'You look lovely. Go on, have a good time.'

'Are you sure you don't mind me going without you?'

'Heavens, no. I've been hundreds of times. I'd much rather read my book. Go on, off you go; don't keep Charles waiting.'

'All right, I'll come and tell you all about it when I come back, shall I?' With a little grin, excitement shining in her brown eyes, she slipped out.

The need for effort gone, Melly stared blindly at the door. She felt bereft.

When Jean-Marc brought her up her tray she was still staring miserably ahead of her. Anything else seemed too much effort, including eating. When he returned for the tray he tutted, as he always tutted when she didn't eat properly, and handed her the hot milk he had made without, for once, being asked. He went away looking gloomy. Poor Jean-Marc. She feared she was a sore trial to him.

The milk drunk, she had a quick shower and got into her nightdress. She was still awake when Nita tapped softly on her door at gone midnight.

'Still awake?'

Desperately trying to infuse brightness into her voice, she insisted, 'Yes, of course. Did you have a good time?'

'Oh, yes.' As she exclaimed over recognising this famous face or that, exclaimed over the dresses, the jewellery, the dishy men, Melly remained quiet, a faint smile pinned firmly to her face. 'And Alison Marks, the actress, actually spoke to me! He knows them all, doesn't he?' she added more quietly. 'I can't believe ... I mean, it seems so odd that my friend Melly is his wife. Aren't you just the tiniest bit in awe of him?'

Surprised, she shook her head, then, thinking about it, she wondered if it wasn't perhaps because she only ever saw him, not the lifestyle. Certainly she had never felt intimidated. To her he was just Charles. For years he had filled her life to the exclusion of all else so that perhaps she was incapable of being detatched, incapable of seeing him as he really was. 'Were you intimidated?' she asked curiously.

'Yes, a bit, I think. He's so—well, worldly, I suppose. Sophisticated. Like the people you read about in magazines. I had to keep pinching myself to make sure it was real. But he was very kind, and patient. He even showed me how to play the tables.'

'I'm glad. Did you break the bank?' Melly teased.

Shaking her head, she gave a faint smile, 'No, I only put a little bit down; I'm not really a gambler, but I enjoyed watching other people.'

'Charles stayed with you?' she queried, just the tiniest bit worried that he might not have understood Nita's nervousness, although she should have known better, she supposed.

'Oh, yes—well, he only left me for a minute while he went to have a word with someone called Nikko.'

'Mm, along with Charles, and a couple of others, he's one of the shareholders in the casino.'

'Charles is a shareholder?' she exclaimed. 'Gosh.' Perching on the edge of the bed, she continued in her usual ham-fisted fashion, 'It's a whole different world, isn't it? Casinos and racehorses. Yachts. I'm glad for you,' she said earnestly, 'but I don't envy you. I don't think I could cope with it all. And yet you seem to, as though you were born to it.'

'Do I?' she asked, surprised. 'I only behave as I've always behaved I think.'

'Ye-es, but with assurance. Oh, I don't know, it's hard to explain. Maybe it's the smart clothes and the expensive hair-do...'

'Maybe. Although I'm still the same person underneath.'

'Yes, I know. That's what's so nice.' Her face thoughtful for a moment, she added, 'And Charles is nice too, isn't he? Not a show-off, or anything.'

'No.' Her heart heavy, she prayed that Nita would leave it there, not elucidate. A prayer wasted.

Still looking faintly worried, she continued, 'I mean, anyone else would have blamed me, been cold, but he wasn't. He couldn't have been kinder, and that makes me feel worse in a way. I tried to make it right for you before we went out, but he just smiled and told me not to worry. It will be all right, won't it?' she pleaded.

'Of course it will.'

'Only I couldn't bear it if I'd messed it up for you ...'

'You haven——'

'Because I couldn't help sort of noticing that he slept in another room last night.'

Oh, Nita, Nita.

'And he still seems a bit distant with you, if you know what I mean. Not rude, or impolite or anything, just a bit cool, and not talking to you very much,' she added with a little frown.

'When has he had a chance to talk to me?' Melly managed to ask lightly. 'We were out all day, and now you've been out with him all evening. Anyway, he can talk to me any old time. The important thing is for you to have a good time. And as for him being cool, I think you're imagining it. I haven't noticed,' she lied. 'And he's sleeping in the spare room because I find it difficult to get comfortable at the moment, so this way he at least gets his sleep. I'm sorry if you've been worrying about it, and if I've seemed a party pooper it isn't anything to do with Charles. The truth is I find it difficult to stand for long periods at the moment, and, tame as it might sound, I was more than grateful to just stay home and rest.'

'Honest?'

'Honest,' she confirmed firmly. 'Now, it's late; go and get your beauty sleep—you can tell me the rest tomorrow.' And Melly might have known that Nita would put the wrong interpretation on her words.

'Oh!' she exclaimed with a little blush. 'I expect I'm keeping him from saying goodnight to you.'

What else could she say but 'yes'?

Much to her surprise, he did come in, and readily informed her why. 'For appearances' sake. Nita was clearly expecting it.' His face was sombre, his eyes bleak, and that, more than anything else, might be the one thing to destroy her, she thought. It was difficult to blame him, or hate him, when she knew he was hurting too.

More to break the awful silence than because she really had anything to say, she murmured, 'Nita had a good time, she said.'

'Did you expect different? None of this is her fault.'

'No,' she agreed miserably, 'it's just that she can't cope with tension, she gets upset.' Which was why it was always so difficult to give her a crushing reply, blame her when she said something out of turn, because she always took it to heart, always became anguished. 'Thank you for taking her.'

He still had not moved from his position by the door, and after staring at her for a few minutes, and still without answering, he turned and went out.

*   *   *

Nita spent three more days with them. Days of
torment for Melly as she fought to act the role of
a contented wife and mother-to-be. Fought to smile,
act naturally.

They took her to the charming town of Honfleur,
spent a leisurely day looking at the shops, sitting
in one of the outside cafés by the harbour, watching
the world go by. Charles took her to see his horses,
and promised that she could return to see them race
the following year when they were old enough, and,
hopefully, trained enough. What he didn't tell her
was that Melly probably wouldn't be there as her
hostess.

On the last morning Melly took her into
Deauville, and, despite Nita's constant exclamations at the prices in the exclusive shops, she bought
her a beautiful scarf from Yves St Laurent.

'But Melly,' Nita protested, 'I can't accept this!
It's far too expensive!'

'Nonsense! Don't you like it?'

'Like it? Like it?' she exclaimed comically. 'It's
exquisite!'

'Then stop complaining!'

'I'm not complaining, you know I'm not. But,
Melly, it cost almost a month's wages!'

Laughing, she hugged her friend. 'Don't exaggerate. It was nice to see you.' Kissing her on the
cheek, she added gently, 'Thank you for coming.'

'You really didn't mind?'

'No, we really didn't mind.'

'And I can come again? When the baby's born?'

'Yes, of course.' What else could she say? No?
That, due to your meddling, Charles and I will no

longer be together once the baby's born? No, unthinkable.

They stood together to wave Nita off, present a united front. As soon as the car was out of sight Charles said flatly, 'I shall be going away in the morning.'

Unable for a moment to take in what he had said, she just stared at him. 'Away?' she echoed unhappily.

'Yes.'

Why? Because he could no longer stand the sight of her? Yet what else had she expected? That they would play happy families until the baby was born? With a sinking heart, she asked miserably, 'Am I allowed to know where?'

After a small hesitation he admitted, 'Monte Carlo.'

She felt so sick for a moment that she couldn't speak. Monte Carlo—and the power-boat racing that was due to start in a few weeks' time. Every season someone was killed, or maimed. Even this year, there had already been two casualties during the practice trials, and he'd promised that he wouldn't race; but that was before he'd found out she was a cheat. It took enormous effort to form words, a sentence, but she finally managed it. 'How long will you be away?'

'I don't know. A few weeks. I'll be back before the baby's born.'

If you're still alive. Swallowing hard, she murmured huskily, 'I thought you'd given up your place to someone else.'

'I did, but Nikko's co-pilot has broken his leg. I offered to replace him.'

'The other night,' she commented emptily, knowing she was right. Nita had said he'd left her in the casino for a few minutes to have a word with Nikko.

'You never know, you might end up a wealthy widow——'

'Don't,' she said thickly. 'Dear God, don't say that!' Feeling the blood drain from her face, she swayed and would have fallen if he hadn't been there to support her.

With an exclamation of concern—or irritation—he put one arm round her waist and helped her inside to the lounge. 'Sit down, I'll get you a drink. Tea, or something,' he added vaguely.

Leaning back in her chair, she closed her eyes and fought to dispel pictures of broken limbs; of horrific injuries; of a blood-soaked body being brought ashore. They went at such fantastic speeds that they only had to hit a wave, a piece of debris...

'Here,' he said roughly, 'drink this.'

Opening her eyes, she stared blindly at the balloon glass and the brandy it contained.

'I can't,' she protested faintly, 'it will make me sick.'

With a long sigh he put the glass on the side-table. 'Jean-Marc is making you some tea,' he added tiredly. Walking away from her, he stood, hands in pockets, legs astride, staring out into the garden. 'I'm sorry. I didn't mean to upset you.'

Staring at him, still feeling the most awful pre-monition of disaster, she pleaded faintly, 'Don't go.'

'I have to. I gave my word.'

And Charles would never go back on his word. But if he hadn't given it? Would he have backed out? Because she'd asked him to? 'Take Jean-Marc with you,' she urged.

Swinging round in astonishment, he asked, 'Whatever for?'

'I don't know,' she admitted helplessly. 'To look after you or something.'

'Don't be ridiculous! I'll be fine. I'm always fine.'

Yes, he was. But one day the luck would run out. And what on earth was it that had made him so hell-bent on his own destruction? What was it that made a man want to pit his wits and skill against whatever challenge came along? Boredom? Lack of self-worth? And yet, on the surface, neither of those things seemed to apply to Charles.

With an abrupt movement that made her start he demanded forcefully, 'What did you expect, Melly? That I would forgive and forget? Tell you that I didn't mind being used? Well, I do mind,' he gritted almost savagely. 'I mind like hell! I liked you! Trusted you! And now I find I can't even bear to be near you without wanting to smash something! I feel—unclean! I look at you and I wonder what's going on behind that quiet face! I examine everything you do or say, looking for traps! Well, I can't live like that! Don't *want* to live like that! As soon as the baby's born we'll go our separate ways. I don't think I ever want to see you again!' Breathing heavily, he strode across the room and slammed out.

Feeling shocked, her nerves ragged, she was still shaking when Jean-Marc came in a few minutes later with her tea.

With a look of compassion, he set the tray down beside her. 'I gather he told you.'

'About the race?' she managed shakily. 'Yes.'

'He'll be all right.'

'Yes,' she agreed without conviction. She had never seen him so angry. So impassioned.

'I do not know what I can say, how I can help...' he began helplessly.

'No.'

'Such a fool as he is. Come, drink your tea,' he added gently.

Fool? No, he wasn't a fool, just an angry and disillusioned man.

When she got up the next morning he'd already gone. No note, no message, just gone. For the second time since their marriage, she breakfasted alone. A sample of what was to come? A future without Charles? Staring at the fresh croissants in their snowy napkin, she began to cry. Tears ran silently down her white face and dripped on to the backs of her hands. There was such a big ache inside of her for this one man, and no way to express it. Unable to hold him, have him hold her in return, was slowly destroying her, especially as it might nearly have been so perfect.

Without Nita's presence to distract her she thought she might go mad. There was no one to confide in, no one to offer comfort, and she spent her days trailing listlessly round the house. She went for another scan, and, by luck, the doctor was not there, and could therefore not insist she stay in as he had threatened. The midwife, reluctantly, it seemed, admitted that there was no reason for her not to go home, so long as she rested. And the weeks slipped by. Weeks without Charles, and if it hadn't been for Jean-Marc she often wondered whether she would have got through it. His concern and kindness was balm to her troubled spirit. He mothered her. Teased her. Encouraged her, and gently reproved her when she snapped at him.

'You really must not cry so much, *madame*. It is not good for the baby. Why not go back to bed for a while?'

'I don't want to go back to bed! I'm sick of bed!' Glaring at him, she suddenly burst into tears.

'And that's enough of that as well,' he said awkwardly. 'Think of the little one!'

Averting her face and sniffing, she muttered, 'I do think of the little one. And if you didn't creep around all the time, making me jump...' Staring at his hurt face, she smiled. 'Sorry.' If there was one thing he didn't do, it was creep.

'So I should think. Now, go into the diningroom; I will bring your breakfast.'

'I'm not hungry...'

'Then you should be.' Opening the dining-room door, he ushered her inside. Five minutes later he came in with her breakfast. Placing a croissant on her plate, he commanded her to eat. Picking up both jugs, he poured first milk, and then a dash of coffee into her cup. 'Drink. When do you go back to hospital?' he enquired gently.

'Tomorrow.'

'I will come——'

'Don't be silly. I can go on my own.'

'Can,' he acceded with a faint smile for her foolishness, 'but won't. What time?'

Her face set, she glanced up at him. Encountering his bland expression, she sighed and gave in. 'Ten.'

'Is good. You can have the sleep-in.'

'Thanks,' she said drily. 'Your kindness is overwhelming.'

'*Oui*,' he agreed, straight-faced. 'It overwhelms me too sometimes.'

'Oh, go away.'

With a contented smile, he obeyed.

At nine-thirty the next morning he helped her into the car, fitted her seatbelt carefully over her lump, closed the door, walked round to the driver's side, and got in. 'You have drunk your one and half pints?'

'You know very well I have. You stood over me while I did so.'

'Mm. You have your card?'

'Yes.'

'Sample?'

Turning her head, she just looked at him.

With a little chuckle, he switched on the engine and put the car in gear.

For some reason best known to himself, he was enjoying himself. Why? And she had still never found out what the relationship was between himself and her husband. Because if Charles hadn't inherited him along with the house, which had apparently not been won in a poker game, then who exactly was Jean-Marc? And where had he come from? And somehow he just didn't seem the sort of man to enjoy washing dishes, making beds, and cooking.

'Why?' she asked.

'Why what?'

'Why do you work for us?'

Looking surprised, he asked, 'You do not think I should?'

'No!' she exclaimed. 'I didn't mean that. I meant, well, you don't seem ... well, you don't seem as I imagine a butler should seem.'

'I don't?' he asked in obvious amusement.

'No.'

'Oh. You think I should take lessons?' he asked blandly.

Never one to waste energy on a lost cause, she pulled a face and lapsed into silence.

'I will wait,' he said when he halted outside the hospital.

'I might be a long time,' she warned.

With another of his odd smiles he insisted quietly, 'I will still wait.'

With a little shrug she turned to go in. An enigma, that's what he was. A puzzle. How much did he know, or suspect, about her relationship with Charles? He must have known of the disagreement between them, yet he had never mentioned it, never gave any intimation of awareness. Why? Because he wasn't interested? Or because he didn't think it was part of his duties? Knowing that her speculation was merely a mask for her nervousness about the forthcoming scan, and that the nearer she got to the clinic, the harder it would be to distract herself, she switched her mind to thought of Charles. What was he doing now? This very minute? Did he think about her? The baby? Which brought her right back to her worries. It would be fine, she tried to convince herself. The baby would have grown; everything would be all right. With the worry over Charles overshadowing her worries for the baby during the last week, she had managed to push the doctor's words to the back of her mind, but now, as she rode up in the lift, her fear returned.

She didn't have long to wait, fortunately, and was almost immediately shown into the cubicle and helped on to the bed.

Staring at the monitor, then at the nurse's face, she tried to interpret both.

'Is it all right?'

'*Oui*,' she answered pleasantly. Helping Melly off the couch, she handed her her card and ushered her out to the reception desk before calling her next patient.

'Ah, Madame Revington. 'Ow are you?'

'Fine, thank you. I have to go down to be monitored?'

'*Oui*, and to see Doctor. Do not look so—agitated. It will be fine.'

Except it wasn't.

'We want you in,' Dr Lafage insisted.

'But why? The baby's fine—you said so!'

'I also said it was small! I am sorry, but it is best to be safe than sorry. Yes? We wish for you to have complete rest, good meals, and also to have a Dopla scan.'

'Which is what?'

'It will show if baby is getting the—er—nutrients, that the supply of goodness to the baby is not blocked in any way. You understand? We need to find a reason why baby is not growing. You are thirty-four weeks, but the baby is only the size of thirty weeks. So, no arguments, young lady; you are coming in. Today.'

Staring at him, so many fears crowding her mind, desperately needing reassurance, she asked faintly, 'What happens if it doesn't grow?'

'Then we will do a Caesarian section.'

'But is thirty-four weeks old enough for the baby to survive?' she asked worriedly.

'Of course.' Leaning across his desk, he patted her hand. 'Trust me, *madame*. But for the baby's sake, and yours, we must have you in so that we can monitor progress. And then, if we think it necessary... Also,' he added with the harassed air of a man who decided it would be best to get all the bad news over at once, 'it is still breech. It may turn, of course, but...'

'But if it doesn't, and it doesn't grow...'

'Yes. I am sorry. But the heart is strong, the limbs full of energy, I think—I am sure,' he qualified, 'that it is just a small baby.'

But not totally, she thought.

'Your husband is with you today?'

'No,' she whispered.

'Ah. There is someone else who may help? Yes? Good. It might be best to bring all the baby things in with you, just in case. If you will speak to the nurse outside she will book a bed for you. Tell you what time to return. Yes?'

With a tired nod she got to her feet. Feeling choked and afraid, knowing that if she tried to say more she would burst into tears, she walked blindly out to the car park without seeing the nurse. If all the nutrients weren't getting through, would the baby be brain damaged? Spastic? Should she ring her mother? No, she'd be worried sick; best not to tell her... Leaning against the wall, she fought for composure. Supposing it died? Supposing...?

'*Madame*! Ah, *madame*, what is it?' Jean-Marc asked gently from beside her.

As she stared at him without really seeing him, her bottom lip quivered.

'It is the baby?'

She gave a little nod.

'It is not well?'

Shaking her head, she gulped, and then the tears came. A great flood of them as she cried out all the worry, and hurt, and pain. The anguish over the baby; her misery over the break with Charles; and, once started, she couldn't seem to stop. Just sobbed on Jean-Marc's shoulder as though her heart would break.

CHAPTER SIX

'Hush, hush, don't cry any more.' Moving slightly, Jean-Marc handed Melly his handkerchief. 'Come, now, dry your eyes and tell me.'

Blowing her nose hard, and wiping the tears away, she gave him a rather garbled account of what the doctor had said.

'And you have seen the nurse?'

'No,' she whispered.

'Then come. You will sit comfortably in the car, and I will make enquiries.'

Waiting in the car, absently shredding Jean-Marc's handkerchief, she tried to think positive thoughts. Hadn't Victoire told her that the doctor had said the same to her? And she'd had no trouble. Now had beautiful twin girls. But twins were always small...

'Stop right there!' Jean-Marc said firmly as he climbed in beside her. 'To worry and fret will not help the baby! Now is no time to think of yourself! You understand?'

'Yes,' she whispered meekly.

'*Bien*. First we will go shopping, buy the things necessary for the little one. Then we will go home, you will have a nice warm bath while I pack your things. You will then eat some lunch——'

'I couldn't...'

'You can, and will. Jean-Marc has said so. Without Charles here to make you do these things

101

then it must be I who does them. No more arguments. It is understood?'

With another little sniff she nodded.

'*Bien.*'

It was Jean-Marc who chose the baby things. Little vests, bootees, disposable nappies, soap, towel, talc. Everything, in fact, that he thought a baby might need. It was Jean-Marc who collected brochures of cots, prams, cribs. 'So that,' he explained patiently, 'when the little one is born, you can choose which you want for the nursery.'

'Yes,' she agreed listlessly, and, if the shop assistants wondered at her apathy, let them wonder. The happy mother-to-be, she thought on a caught sob.

'That is quite enough of that. The baby is going to be fine!' Holding her by the shoulders, he stared deep into her eyes. 'Say it! The baby is going to be fine!'

'The baby is going to be fine,' she whispered.

'*Bien.* Now we will go home.'

He drove them the short distance to the house, hustled her upstairs, ran her bath. Waited patiently while she collected clean underwear and a clean dress, then firmly closed the bathroom door on her.

Lying in the warm, scented water, her toes on the taps, she stared up at the ceiling. She wanted Charles. What was he doing now? Suited up, ready to race? Laughing with Nikko? Not a care in the world? Had he remembered she had a hospital visit today? When was the race? She couldn't remember. Perhaps he was already dead. Perhaps he had crashed in practice . . . The loud knock on the bathroom door made her jump.

'Come along, *madame*. Do not go to sleep in the bath.'

'Coming,' she called automatically. 'Five minutes.'

Fatalism hung about her like a cloud when she emerged from the bathroom, and Jean-Marc sighed. 'I do not know what to do, or say, to make it better,' he confessed unhappily.

'No.' With a wan little smile she pushed her feet into her shoes. 'I'm ready.'

'Lunch first—no arguments. A little soup, for the baby's sake.'

'Yes, for the baby's sake. And, Jean-Marc?' she added as he seated her at the table. 'You're not to tell Charles.'

'But——'

'No.' She'd thought about it, considered it fully while she'd been in the bath, and had come to the conclusion that she didn't want him told. If he was committed to race, which he was, she wanted his full attention on what he was doing, not on the baby. It wouldn't be on her, she knew, but he would worry about the baby, his baby, and she didn't want him distracted in any way. Power-boat racing was dangerous enough when you had all your concentration on the task; it could be fatal if you didn't. 'Promise, Jean-Marc.'

With obvious reluctance, he nodded. 'I promise. He will be angry when he finds out. With us both.'

'No,' she denied, 'not angry. Hurt, maybe, but not angry.'

With a little shrug, he indicated for her to begin on her soup.

Far too soon Jean-Marc delivered her to the hospital. He escorted her up to her room, handed her over to the nurse, and left, promising to return that evening.

Over the next few days a routine was set up. She was prodded, poked, weighed, monitored, made to rest, made to get up, and, apart from the worry and anguish over the baby and Charles, her chief emotion was boredom. Jean-Marc had installed a portable television in her room, but, seeing as every programme was naturally in French, and Melly's French was hardly proficient, she soon grew bored with trying to work out what was going on. Apart from which she was terrified of accidentally seeing the power-boat race. She still didn't know what day the race was taking place. Nor did she want to. She wanted to pretend it wasn't happening.

In desperation Jean-Marc bought her knitting needles and wool and a selection of patterns. She hadn't liked to tell him that she couldn't knit. One of the nurses tried to teach her, but she got in such a mess, and she was hardly likely to put her baby in the holey, tangled thing she ended up with. If the baby was all right.

She had no visitors, apart from Jean-Marc, because no one knew she was in there. She hadn't wanted anyone to know. She did not think she could have borne expressions of sympathy, confident exclamations that all would be well; she needed to come to terms with it in her own way. Needed to prepare herself for the worst. Anyway, she wasn't very good at talking about her feelings, she never had been. Even when Donny had died, only Charles had ever understood what was in her heart. Why couldn't he understand now?

Her parents had shut themselves off, somehow failing to understand that Melly's grief had been as real as their own, so she'd had to pretend to be strong for their sakes. Only Charles had not needed explanations; after the funeral, when all the mourners had gone home, he had come, taken her out in his car, held her, let her cry, and for the rest of the week he had remained in Beckford, her sole source of comfort. Had that been the real beginning of her love for him? Because he alone had seemed to care? Understand a fifteen-year-old's pain and bewilderment? Or was it because he was already a god to her? Already an object of hero-worship? And, in her confusion and bewilderment, had she endowed him with powers he didn't possess? Seen him in a distorted light? Yet when had that hero-worship turned to love? So hard, now, to know. So hard to remember that far back.

Closing her eyes, she tried to recall how it had been. How he had been. At what age had she known it was love? At sixteen, when he had given her her first, very gentle, chaste kiss? At eighteen, when he had taken her out for the evening to wine and dine her? It had been avuncular, she knew that, but had it been then that she had fallen in love with him? She didn't know; it just felt as though it had always been there. Was it habit? Is that what it was? Or was it simply a first love that had never faded?

With a long sigh, no nearer knowing the answer than she had ever been, she picked up her pad and attempted to finish the children's story that she had been struggling with since her marriage. Good job it hadn't been a commission.

There were three other women in adjoining rooms, none of whom spoke English, so the most that were ever exchanged were nods and smiles. Only one of the nurses spoke English, but she was usually busy and could only spare a few minutes each day to chat, until the following week, when she accompanied Dr Lafage.

'So, *madame*,' he beamed, 'we have decided.'

Feeling suddenly cold and shivery, she asked carefully, 'Decided what?'

'Two days from now you will be thirty-six weeks, so we have decided to wait no longer. Baby is still breech, and still quite small, but we think now about five of your English pounds. So, a Caesarian, I'm afraid. You will wish for an epidural or anaesthetic?'

An epidural was an injection into the spine, and she'd heard some pretty horrific stories about those. But an anaesthetic meant she would be unconscious, and so would not know until an hour or so later whether the baby was all right.

'No need to decide now,' he said kindly. 'Nurse will come back later and explain it all to you. Now, let's have a little listen.'

When the nurse had pulled up her nightie he produced what looked like an old-fashioned ear trumpet, and placed the cold metal on her tummy, making her flinch. Bending, he put his ear to the other end and listened for a few moments. So much for modern technology, she thought with a flicker of amusement. Didn't he trust the monitor?

Straightening, he beamed, said something to the nurse in his own tongue, and left.

'Don't worry, I'll come back later,' the nurse said hastily before hurrying after him.

Don't worry. No. Easy for her to say. Whether it had been the cold metal, her nervousness, or some other reason, the baby began to make violent protest, and she smiled. At least it was active; that was a good sign, wasn't it?

She debated long and hard about whether to tell Jean-Marc, but decided in the end that she had better. Although the hospital had details of her next of kin, both Charles and her parents, if anything happened Jean-Marc would at least have first-hand knowledge.

'So,' he smiled, 'in a few days you will be a *maman*?'

'Yes, I hope so.'

Perching on the edge of the bed, he picked up her hand. 'And so now we must tell Charles,' he said softly.

Looking away from brown eyes that always seemed to see too much, she picked at the blanket. 'Is the race over?' she asked quietly. When he didn't immediately answer she prompted, 'Well? It isn't, is it?'

'*Non*. It is to——'

'No! Don't tell me!' she protested quickly. Leaning back, trying to relax, she once more held his eyes. 'You only tell him when it is over. You promised, Jean-Marc.'

'But only because I thought he would be back well before you had the baby!'

'It doesn't matter why you promised; you did. You're not to tell him until the race is finished. Your word, Jean-Marc.'

With a long sigh he agreed. 'I give it. Reluctantly. But I will ensure that the nurse has my number just in case it is sooner.'

'It won't be sooner,' she said confidently. 'They said Thursday.'

'I will still make sure they have my number.' Watching her quietly for a moment, he added hesitantly, 'He rang, you know, to see if you were all right.'

'Did he?' she managed to ask neutrally. Her insides might flutter and contract at the mention of his name, but for some silly reason she did not want Jean-Marc to know of her eagerness for details.

'Yes. You have forced me to lie, *madame* . . .'

'But you did not tell him?' she demanded urgently.

'No. I did not tell him. I said you were fine, and he said he would ring again in a few days. It is fortunate, is it not, that he did not ask to speak with you?'

Knowing he was still watching her, obviously waiting, she refused to be drawn. What could she say? That of course he had not asked to speak with her? Because he did not care about her? Only the baby? No. Tell no one, Charles had said. 'I expect he was busy,' she commented with the same neutrality.

With a little sigh that in no way dispelled the curiosity lurking in his eyes, he thankfully changed the subject. 'No, first thing in the morning I will make sure that the pram and crib we have ordered are ready for delivery.' Clasping her hand tight, he reassured, 'It will be all right, *madame*. Now, no more worry. Get some sleep; I will see you tomorrow afternoon.'

'All right, and thank you—for everything. I don't know how I would have managed without you.'

'*Ah, pouf*,' he said dismissively. '*Bonsoir*.' With his gentle smile, he left.

Was the race today, or tomorrow? 'To...' he had begun to say. Was it over? Or not yet begun? Thankfully, her thoughts were distracted by the arrival of the monitor, being wheeled into the room by the English-speaking nurse.

'Your friend has left me his number,' she smiled. 'He seemed most concerned. Your husband does not mind that he looks after you while he is away?'

'No,' she said quietly. She hadn't the faintest idea whether Charles minded or not. Probably grateful that he didn't have to do it.

'You will be watching tomorrow for the race?' she asked absently as she linked Melly up to the machine. 'Me, I would be worried sick... *Ah, pardon, madame*!' she exclaimed unhappily. 'I should not have mention—— Now, now, do not be upset, he will be fine. He is very good, very skilled; I have seen him before in the racing.'

Before was before, Melly thought bleakly. This was now. So it was tomorrow. And tomorrow night she might be a widow... Oh, don't be so damned defeatist!

When the nurse had gone she lay back and tried very hard to put it out of her mind, but, with nothing to distract her thoughts, her fears grew and magnified, until she'd almost convinced herself that she *was* a widow. She didn't sleep very well, and in the morning the nurse was sufficiently alarmed by her white face as to fetch the doctor. The baby, too, seemed to be kicking more than usual. Melly was comforted by the activity; not so the nursing staff, and for the rest of that day they monitored her very carefully. At the back of her mind was always the thought of Charles, but her fears were now overshadowed by the worried faces of the staff. At four the doctor returned.

He stood, reading the print-out and her chart, his face thoughtful, then, hooking the chart back on the end of the bed, pronounced in careful English, 'We have the fear that the baby is becoming stressed. We have therefore decided to wait no longer. You had no lunch?'

'No,' she denied slowly, 'the nurse advised against it.' Obviously because she had thought this might happen, Melly realised.

'Then the nurse will get you ready.' With a last smile for her, he spoke quickly to the nurse in his own language, then left.

'Relax,' the nurse said kindly. 'It will be all right. You wish for me to ring your friend?'

'Please.'

Feeling sick and fearful, she remained silent while the nurse got her ready. Was the race over? she wondered. Did Charles now know she was in the hospital? Or was he incapable of knowing anything?

When she opened her eyes Charles was standing at the foot of the bed, his hands clenched on the rail. Staring at him, devouring him almost, she closed her eyes tight in silent gratitude, and only then absorbed his look of anguish. The baby? Oh, no; please, no. Snapping her eyes open again, she croaked fearfully, 'The baby?'

'A girl,' he said thickly. 'She's all right, she...' Breaking off, he swallowed hard and turned his head away for a minute. 'She's all right,' he repeated.

'And you?' she whispered.

'As you see.'

The two things she had most feared now proved groundless, she relaxed, untensed her muscles. 'Did you win?' she asked sleepily.

'No. Go to sleep.'

Obediently closing her eyes, she slept.

When next she woke she wished she hadn't. Her body felt one mass of pain. She was lying on carefully stacked pillows; there was a drip in one arm, and she was thirsty. Carefully turning her head towards the window, she saw Charles seated in the chair. His head was thrown back, his eyes closed. As she turned the other way her eyes filled with tears, seeing the cot drawn up beside the bed. A glass dome hid the pink blanket-wrapped bundle inside. Her baby. A daughter. Trying to lever herself up to see more clearly, she collapsed limply back as pain shot through her stomach.

'Easy,' Charles said quietly, 'you'll have to lie still for a while.'

Turning her head towards him, she complained weakly, 'I'm so thirsty.'

Putting out a hand as though to touch her, he changed his mind and allowed it to fall limply to his side. 'I'm afraid you can't have anything to drink for twenty-four hours.'

'Oh. Is the baby all right?'

'Yes. You asked me that before.'

'Did I?' she asked, confused. 'I don't remember. She's not—damaged or anything?'

'No.' His jaw clenched, his hands tight on the arms of the chair, he suddenly shot to his feet and went to stand at the window, his back to her.

Watching him, wanting him, yearning to be held, she whispered softly, 'Did you win?'

'No. I told you that, too.' Swinging round, he demanded anguishedly, 'Why didn't you tell me? Why? Didn't you think I had a right to know?'

Her eyes filling with helpless tears at his harsh tone, she bit her lip and looked away. 'I didn't want you distracted,' she whispered. 'I've been so worried.'

'Oh, Melly,' he sighed. 'What a God-awful mess.'

Her face still averted, she heard him move, then watched as he walked to stand beside the cot. Looking down, he put his finger carefully beneath the plastic dome and moved the pink blanket aside so that he could see the baby's face. 'She's so small,' he said softly, almost reverently. 'Such a tiny little thing. So perfect.' His voice thick, he carefully replaced the blanket and looked at her. He looked exhausted. His eyes red-rimmed from tiredness and worry, his face grey. He also needed a shave—and he had never looked so dear. 'She is still to be called Lauren?' he asked hesitantly.

'Yes, if you still want to, that is.'

'It is, thank you. Get some sleep; I'll be back later. Jean-Marc sends his love.'

Without answering, she watched him leave, listened to his footsteps retreating down the corridor. No kiss goodbye, no shared joy... Fighting back fresh tears, she reached out her hand and gently manoeuvred the cot nearer to the bed. She wanted to see her. Hold her. She quite desperately needed to do that. That tiny bundle had to be worth the anguish and the pain and the heartache. Had to! Her hand still clenched on the cot rail, she drifted back into sleep.

When next she woke it was dark, and the cot was gone. In panic, she pressed the buzzer. The nurse was there in seconds.

'*Qu'est-ce qu'il y a*?' she queried urgently.

With equal urgency, Melly demanded, 'Where's my baby?'

'*Bébé*? *Ah, oui*,' she grinned as she thankfully relaxed. '*Bébé est en train de...*' Her face screwed up in thought, she finally pronounced, 'Is eating!'

'Oh,' she exclaimed weakly. Feeling stupid, she gave the nurse a sheepish smile. '*Pardon.*'

'*De rien.*' She smiled. 'It does not matter.'

'How long? Er—*combien de temps*?'

With a little shrug, her face all scrumpled, she sucked her teeth and wagged her head from side to side, then pronounced triumphantly, 'Soon!' With a little giggle, she went back to her duties.

Not five minutes later Charles walked slowly and very, very carefully into the room. He held the baby as though he were carrying eggs. His face firmed with concentration, he walked across to the bed, and very gently lowered the baby into Melly's waiting arms.

'Whew!' he exclaimed comically. 'I don't think I have ever been so frightened in my entire life! That wretched nurse made me carry her right along the corridor!'

But Melly was barely listening. This was the first time she had held her daughter, and she needed to savour it. Giving Charles an abstracted smile, and therefore not noticing that he was carefully avoiding her eyes, she stared down at the tiny bundle. 'Oh, Charles,' she exclaimed tearfully, 'she's perfect!'

'Yes.' Seeing her difficulty, and still without looking directly at her face, he bent forward and rearranged one of the pillows so that the baby was supported at her side.

Feeling awkward, and somehow shy with him, she kept her gaze determinedly fixed on the baby. 'Thank you. It's hard to hold her with my tummy so sore.'

'Yes, you'll have to take it easy for a while. Hang on a minute.'

When he walked swiftly out she released a shuddery breath. We sound so stilted with each other, she thought bleakly, so distant, so she was completely taken by surprise when he returned seconds later carrying an enormous bouquet of red roses.

Laying them on the foot of the bed, he stood looking sheepish for a moment, then with a crooked smile he finally faced her, and shrugged.

Staring at them through a blur of tears, she hesitantly raised her eyes to his. Were they from him? How to ask? Or should she just assume? Just assume, she decided; that would be the least embarrassing. 'They're lovely,' she whispered tremulously. 'Thank you.'

'Well, no need to cry,' he said awkwardly. Still staring at her, as though trying to find the right way to say something, he blurted out, 'Melly, I——'

'*Bonsoir*,' Jean-Marc said hesitantly from the doorway, and whatever Charles had been going to say was lost. Advancing into the room, another enormous bouquet cradled in his arms, he quickly congratulated Charles, dropped the flowers into the sink, sidled round the empty cot, and smiled warmly at Melly. 'Congratulations!'

Grateful for the interruption, even if Charles was not, she gave Jean-Marc a warm smile.

Glancing down at the baby, he hesitantly touched one small hand. 'She is exquisite,' he said almost reverently. 'Might I hold her? Just for one small moment?'

With extreme reluctance she relinquished the baby into his hold. 'Don't drop her, will you?' she cautioned, only half jokingly.

'Of course not,' he reassured, and, in truth, he handled the baby much more easily than Charles had done, and she wondered if, perhaps, he had children of his own. Not something she could ask at the moment. 'She is very beautiful,' he pronounced. 'Like her *maman*. How big?'

'Just under five pounds,' Charles informed him coolly. 'And I think she needs to go back into her cot,' he added peevishly.

Looking startled, Jean-Marc turned slowly to face him, and then gave a slow smile. Handing the baby back to Melly, he gave her a little wink. 'I

can see that I am no longer wanted, so I will return
to the home and begin preparations for the nursery.'

'I can do that...' Charles began, but he was
talking to himself; Jean-Marc had already gone.
'Interfering bastard,' he muttered rudely.

Staring at him in astonishment, she looked hastily
away when he glared at her. That was the first time
she had ever heard him be less than polite to his
butler; and, in this instance, undeservedly so.
Perhaps he was just tired. Or feeling possessive over
the baby—and then she remembered what it was
he had said: 'As soon as the baby's born we'll go
our separate ways.'

'Melly?' Charles exclaimed in concern. 'You've
gone as white as a sheet! Here, give me the baby.'
Hurrying round the bed, he carefully took her and
put her gently in the cot. Covering her, he replaced
the plastic dome. 'Shall I get the nurse?'

Shaking her head, she lay tiredly back on the
pillows. 'No, I'm all right.'

'You're in pain,' he pronounced as though he
were an authority on the subject. 'Haven't they
given you anything?' he demanded. 'Well, we'll see
about that!'

'Charles, I'm all right,' she exclaimed wearily,
and found herself talking to empty air. 'I'm just
tired,' she concluded lamely.

He returned with the English-speaking nurse,
who looked at her with concern. 'Too much excitement, too much talking. You need to rest. You
are in very bad pain?'

'N——'

'Yes!' Charles overrode. 'Can you give her
something?'

'But of course, she is to have a pain-killer before we settle her for the night. But if you would like one now...'

'No, later will do. I'm OK.'

'You are not OK, you look like a ghost! Have one now,' he persuaded more gently.

Feeling it was easier to agree than argue, she nodded. 'All right, and then I just want to sleep.'

'Yes, that will be best; you'll feel much better tomorrow!' he said confidently.

Despite her worry, she was amused by his air of competence, which was quite patently a sham, so she smiled at him, and, to her surprise, he grinned back. Just for one brief moment, the old Charles. And then he presumably remembered, as she did, their differences, and the grin died.

'I'll go now, let you rest. Come back in the morning.' And, presumably because the nurse was still there, he bent to kiss her. 'Goodnight. And, Melly? She's lovely, thank you.'

In the morning she felt ten times worse. The effects of the anaesthetic had worn off, but because she felt more alert the pain seemed more pronounced. Unable to get comfortable, restricted by the drip, she felt petulant and irritable.

'You'll feel better when the drip is removed this afternoon and you can have a drink,' the nurse promised. 'Would you like another pain-killer?'

Shaking her head, she turned her face away. She wanted to grizzle, she found. Wanted to be left alone. When the little pink-wrapped bundle was placed beside her tears ran down her face and dripped on to the blanket. What would happen to her when Charles sent her back to Beckford? Oh, hell, had anyone told her parents? Buzzing for the nurse, she asked if she might have the telephone wheeled in.

'When the doctor has been, and the baby is taken for feeding, then yes, of course,' she agreed with a smile. 'Now, be a good girl and stop fretting. Your delightful husband will be here soon, and you don't want him to find you all blotchy from crying, do you?'

'No,' she agreed lamely.

'He is very—concerned,' she smiled. 'He rang late last night, and again this morning to be sure that all was well.'

'Did he? Did he say if he'd told my parents?'

'Not to me, no, but he will be here soon and then you can ask, yes?'

'Sure. Thank you.'

'It is my pleasure. Also, when you are more comfortable, you will be able to start feeding the baby yourself. Yes? Still the baby will need a bottle until your own milk comes through, but trying will encourage it. You understand?'

'Yes, thank you.'

The two weeks in the hospital after the birth went very quickly, and the nearer it got to her release, the more nervous she got. He wouldn't send her home straight away, would he? Surely he would let her stay in France until the baby was old enough to travel? Yes, of course he would. And the iciness with which he had treated her before seemed to have melted a fraction, hadn't it? He'd been in twice every day, admittedly probably only because of the baby, but he had flown her parents over—and told Victoire so that she might come and visit; that must mean he didn't quite hate her, mustn't it?

Jean-Marc had popped in and out, usually after Charles had left, ostensibly to ask her opinion on this or that nursery item, but she guessed that it was really because he was fascinated by the baby. And she was very touched by his continuing kindness. Grateful that someone seemed to care.

When Charles came to collect her, giving expensive chocolates to the staff in thanks, she scrutinised his face to see if she could detect any changes. Examined his smile, and felt a little ray of hope when she could see no sign of the former bleakness in his eyes. Although the true test would come when she was home. There would be no nurses to put a show on for there.

Jean-Marc was waiting with the front door open when they arrived home, a proud smile on his face, as though he were the father. With a flourish he led her upstairs to see the nursery. Charles followed, looking disgruntled.

It was done out beautifully in pastel shades of pink and green, with white wooden furniture, cot, nursing chair, and even a rocking-horse. Mobiles hung from the ceiling, stuffed toys sat proudly on a shelf. The little wardrobe was filled to capacity, she discovered. Sleeping suits, day suits, dresses, coats. Closing the door, she opened the drawers. They too were filled with woollies, bootees, vests, pants. The white nursing box was filled with toiletries, nappies. There was a changing mat, a bath, a baby alarm already fitted. Everything, in fact, that she and the baby would need. Too choked to say anything, she sat in the nursing chair and rocked slowly back and forth, Lauren cradled in her arms. How much more beautiful it would have been with a loving husband to hold her. She was aware that both men watched her, both seemed anxious, but could find no words to express her feelings.

'You like it?' Charles finally asked.

She just nodded.

'There's something else,' he added.

'Else?'

'Mm. Come see.' Taking the baby from her, as though he had been dying to do so ever since they had left the hospital, he walked across to a door that certainly hadn't been there before. 'Jean-Marc, go and make the coffee,' he said peremptorily.

'Certainly, *m'sieu.*' With a smile for Melly, he went back downstairs.

Opening the door, which now led into her bedroom, he stood aside for her to enter first, which she did, and then halted in surprise. 'Oh, Charles!' she exclaimed softly. 'Oh, Charles.' Not sure she could take much more, she looked round her. Everything was peach and white. Gone was the heavy French furniture, the dressing-table, wardrobe, all replaced by light white wood in one continuous fitted unit along one wall. The carpet and curtains were white. The walls peach. The bed, instead of the four-poster she had been used to, was now a tented masterpiece in peach and white. Beside the bed was a white cradle.

On legs that felt weak, she walked across and gave it a gentle push. It moved silently on its rocker. 'I don't know what to say,' she whispered tearfully.

Turning to face him, she gave a tremulous smile. 'It's beautiful. And the nursery.'

Clearing his throat, he said awkwardly, 'I thought—we thought it would be better to have a connecting door to the nursery, for when she's older,' he added even more awkwardly.

'Yes.' Feeling suddenly cold, she tried to read his face. Did he mean all this for her? Or some nanny he was thinking of employing? And, if so, did that mean he expected her to return to Beckford alone? But not yet! He couldn't send her back yet—she was feeding Lauren herself!

I could feed her forever, she thought hysterically. If that was the only way to stay, she would feed her forever!

CHAPTER SEVEN

'OH, MELLY, you look absolutely shattered!' Charles exclaimed worriedly. 'Come on, downstairs; you've done quite enough for one day.'

Settling her in the lounge, he placed the baby in her lap, and then just continued to look thoughtfully down at her. 'Damn,' he muttered softly.

Staring at him in surprise, she then looked round in an effort to discover what had caused his displeasure. Seeing nothing, she asked, 'What?'

Without answering, he shouted, 'Jean-Marc?'

'*Oui, m'sieu,*' Jean-Marc answered with the weary acceptance of one who expected nothing else but hassle. Placing the coffee on the little table beside Melly's chair, he turned a bland face to Charles.

'We forgot the basket.'

'Basket?'

'Yes, dammit! Melly can't keep carrying the baby round, and she won't want to leave her upstairs during the day—she won't be able to hear her cry! We need one of those carry-cot things!'

'Ah.'

'Moses basket,' Melly put in quietly.

'Ah,' Jean-Marc said again.

Unable to repress the little twitch of her lips, she looked down.

'I'd best go and get one,' Charles murmured with an uncharacteristic lack of decision.

'No need,' Jean-Marc refuted politely, 'I will telephone to the shop and get one delivered. *Vite*.' Walking across to the telephone, he lifted the receiver and began to punch out the digits. 'I know the number by head.'

'Heart,' Charles corrected absently. Turning back to Melly, he gave her a comical smile. 'Here, I'll hold the baby while you drink your coffee.'

Handing her over, she watched as he backed up to the sofa and sat carefully down. He looked to be absolutely fascinated by his daughter. His eyes on her face, he extended his finger to one pink little fist. When she grasped it he beamed proudly. 'Look! She's going to be really strong!'

Glancing at Jean-Marc, and then away again, she obediently drank her coffee. Oh, Charles, how can I ever bear to leave you?

Five minutes later the doorbell rang. 'I'll get it,' Jean-Marc said, 'I expect it is the basket.' But it wasn't; it was Nikko.

Advancing into the room, a short, well-muscled young man, a few years younger than Charles, he stood, hands on hips, in the doorway. 'So, I have come to see this baby that has disrupted my life and cost me the championship! I hope she is worth it!'

'She is,' Charles said softly. 'Come and see.'

Walking across, he stared down at the tiny bundle. 'Hm. Not very big, is she?'

'Well, of course she isn't very big! She's only two weeks old!'

Turning to Melly, Nikko grimaced, then came to perch on the arm of her chair. 'Me, I know nothing about babies—and you have lousy timing, *madame*.'

'I do?'

'*Oui*! Ten minutes more and it would have been too late for recall, and I would now perhaps be the world champion!'

Frowning, she looked up at him. 'I don't understand. I'm very sorry that you didn't win...'

'To win, *madame*,' he said caustically, 'one has to take part!'

'You didn't take part?' she queried in confusion. 'But why?'

'Precisely!' he approved. 'I knew you were a woman of sense! I told him you would not mind— didn't I?' he demanded of Charles. 'But would he listen? No!'

Thoroughly bewildered, she looked at her husband. 'You didn't race?'

'No.' Continuing to test the baby's strong grip, he added with suspect casualness, 'The message to say that you were about to have the baby came just before the start.'

'So you abandoned?'

'Of course.'

Of course? There was no 'of course' about it. 'You didn't say...' Suddenly switching her gaze to Jean-Marc, she protested, 'I asked you not to tell him till after the race. You promised, Jean-Marc!'

Before Jean-Marc could defend himself Nikko spoke for him. 'It wasn't his fault. It was that imbecile of a steward. He took the message, saying to tell Charles after the race, left it on his desk, and some officious busybody found it, decided it was urgent and rushed it to the start line!'

Putting a hand on his knee, she said softly, 'Oh, Nikko, I'm so sorry. I know how much it meant to you.'

'Oh, well, there is always next year,' he said with an about change. With a smile, he patted her hand. 'Not to worry. At least I bring him back safe, hm?'

'Yes. Thank you.' And that, to her, was more important than anything else. Glancing at Jean-Marc, she pulled a little face. 'Sorry, Jean-Marc.'

'No problem.'

Nobody quite liked to ask him why he had not phoned through after the race. And, even if they had, Melly doubted they would have got a satisfactory answer. For all his pretended deference, he was still a law unto himself.

'Well, I'm off,' Nikko said as he got to his feet. Looking over at Charles and the baby, he grinned, then began to laugh. 'Oh, my friend, how the mighty are fallen.' Still chuckling, he went out, accompanied by Jean-Marc.

Watching Charles, as he in turn watched the now sleeping baby, she said softly, 'I'm sorry about the race.'

Looking up, a faint smile in his eyes, he shook his head. 'I'm not. Baby daughters are much more important than titles.'

'You could still have raced——'

'No, Melly,' he said firmly. 'I could not.'

Why? she wanted to ask, but didn't have the courage.

For the next two weeks, during all the midwife's visits, and the doctor's, the baby was as good as gold. As soon as the visits ceased she apparently decided enough was enough. Crying brought attention. Crying got you picked up and cuddled. And to cry at two o'clock in the morning was apparently the best time of all.

'Are you sure there's nothing wrong with her?' Charles demanded. 'Perhaps she's still hungry.'

'She is not still hungry!' Melly retorted irritably.

'Wind, then! Tummy ache...'

'Charles! Go away! Go get some sleep!'

'Sleep? How can I sleep, knowing you aren't getting any? How can I sleep with that racket going on? Here, give her to me, perhaps I can get her off.'

'Then I suggest you remove your jacket, otherwise she's liable to be sick all down it,' she added with a rather malicious satisfaction.

'Oh, charming.'

Shrugging out of his dinner jacket and slinging it across the foot of her bed, he undid his bow tie and left it dangling loosely round his neck. Taking the baby and wrapping her more securely in her blanket, he urged, 'Now, you close your eyes for your daddy. And you,' he added to Melly, 'snuggle under the covers and get some sleep.'

With a thankful sigh, she did as she was told. Her eyes still open, she watched him walk up and down, rocking the crying baby in his arms. He looked—stunning. Dishevelled, and impossibly attractive. This was the third time he'd come into her room after returning from the casino. The first time he'd been very hesitant, knocking carefully and waiting until she'd told him to come in. The second time he'd merely knocked and entered, and tonight had done neither, just walked in, and to say she was astonished by the change in him since the baby's birth would have been an understatement. She had always known he was kind, and, although sometimes it was of the offhand variety, it was none the less meant. But, from a lifestyle where mostly he only needed to please himself, could afford to command others to do what he didn't want to do, he astonished Melly by the time and patience he expended on his daughter. And the enjoyment he seemed to derive from it. Not only, like most men, when she was sleeping, or contented, but when she was being impossible, like now.

But were his actions and his visits really only prompted by concern for the baby? Or was he practising for when he would need to manage without herself? Although surely, if that were the case, he would have insisted on getting a nanny? Or was he just waiting until Lauren went on the bottle and then intended to manage by himself? Not something she was going to ask. So long as she was here, and no one said anything to the contrary, she would keep quiet, and pray. Closing her eyes, she slept.

Already fully attuned to the baby, she woke at the first little murmur. Peering at the clock, she saw it was half-past five. With a groan she rolled over to reach into the cot and encountered an obstacle in the way. A large, warm obstacle. Stretching out her arm, she carefully switched on the bedside lamp. Charles was half sitting, half lying on the edge of the bed. His head was at a most awkward and uncomfortable-looking angle, and his hand was still on the cradle rail, where presumably he had been rocking it before he fell asleep. If she moved him, made him more comfortable, in the morning would he then accuse her of engineering it? Trying to seduce him? Cheat? With a tired sigh she slipped carefully from the bed and walked round to pick up the baby before she could begin crying in earnest and wake him.

Making soothing little noises, she climbed back into bed. Stuffing the pillow behind her, Melly opened her nightdress and began to feed her. Leaning her head back, she closed her eyes, and therefore didn't see Charles wake; didn't see him carefully turn his head to watch her, his eyes confused for a moment until he realised where he was. Only knew when he stirred, gave a funny little sigh, slid down the bed and promptly went back to sleep. Watching him as she continued to feed Lauren, she found the heaven-sent opportunity to touch him too hard to resist. Putting out her hand, she carefully moved her fingers across his hair, down to his stubbled cheek and come to rest on his neck. When he mumbled something in his sleep she froze, and then carefully continued her exploration. It had been such a long time since she had felt his warmth, heard his even breathing from beside her. Such a long, long time, and she wanted desperately to snuggle down beside him, hold him in her arms, touch her mouth to his. Such a nice mouth, so inviting, slightly parted, and a warm ache began in her groin.

Switching the baby, who protested loudly at being moved, to the other breast, she moved her hand to his chest, felt the steady rise and fall, felt his heartbeat. Her eyes pricking with tears, she moved her hand back to the warmth of his neck, let her fingers rest on the pulse beating strongly there. 'I love you,' she whispered. 'Dear God, how I love you. Don't send me away; please let me stay.'

Sliding down the bed, the baby still suckling, she turned on her side and began to cry softly.

She must have fallen asleep, because she woke some hours later to find Charles curved at her back, and the baby still cradled, fast asleep, at her front. Not wanting to move, wishing she could stay here forever, between the two people she loved best in the world, she went back to sleep.

When she woke properly at gone nine Charles was gone, and the baby was demanding to be fed.

He didn't mention the incident when she saw him later, and neither did she. But she did wonder if Jean-Marc knew, because he seemed to be wearing a very satisfied air. She had no idea what he made of their marriage, had never liked to ask, but over the next few weeks she began to feel as though she were walking on eggshells. Frightened of saying or doing anything that might remind Charles that she was only a guest in his house, she said, and did, nothing.

Her mother rang constantly, wanting to see the baby. Wanting to know when Melly was coming back to Beckford for a visit.

'You know Daddy's reluctant to leave the works, now that at long last it's beginning to pick up again, and you know I don't like travelling by myself, so when, Melly?'

'Soon,' she promised. As she always promised. It wasn't that she didn't want to go, just that she was afraid that, if she did, Charles might not want her back.

'Your mother again?' he asked with a smile as she replaced the phone.

'Yes.'

'Poor Mother,' he mocked softly. 'Why not put her out of her misery? Why not go over for a few days? Jacques can fly you over——'

'Oh, no,' she interrupted hastily. 'Not just yet. I'll go next month...'

'Well, it's up to you, of course, but it's only natural that your mother should want to see you. I'll ring Jacques, shall I?'

He seemed very eager for her to go, she thought bleakly as she watched him lift the phone. And had he now decided he didn't want the baby either? Lost in her own miserable thoughts, she didn't listen to his telephone conversation, and only came back to the present when she suddenly became aware that he was talking to her.

'Melly! Wake up! What day do you want to come back?'

'Back?'

'Yes, back!'

Back. The most beautiful word in the English language. Staring at him, suddenly registering his impatience, she said quickly, 'Oh, I don't know, I only want to go for a few days.'

'It's all right for the baby to fly, isn't it?' he queried.

'Oh, yes.'

'Right.' Concluding his conversation with the pilot, he put the phone down. 'OK, that's settled. Jacques is free on Thursday. That gives you two days to get yourself ready. You can spend a long weekend with your parents and come back Tuesday morning. How does that sound?'

'Fine,' she agreed with a cautious smile. Especially the coming-back part.

Jacques was another of his partners. In another venture that seemed to make money. A little charter outfit that flew out of St Gatien. She'd met him a couple of times, and would feel safe flying with him. He was married with two young children, a family man. She didn't know why that was important, but it was. Perhaps it was that if they associated more with family people it might prompt Charles to make his family a real one. Clutching at straws, Melly, she told herself. But they had at least become friends again since the baby was born, hadn't they? He smiled at her again now. Talked to her. But had he forgiven her?

Charles drove her to the airport, saw her safely on board, kissed both her and the baby, told Jacques to take good care of them. He waited, waving, until they took off, and she tried to shake the feeling that she wouldn't be coming back, that this was all a ruse to get rid of them. She had woken up with it that morning, a strange feeling of things changing, coming to an end. Yet she could find nothing in Charles's manner to account for it. He had been as usual, smiling, cheerful, and, if not quite as he had been before Nita's visit, then at least friendly, and no way would he relinquish his little sweetheart, as he called his daughter. No, she was just being silly. But the feeling wouldn't go away.

When she parted from Jacques she emphasised, 'And you will pick me up Tuesday? Charles explained?'

'*Oui, madame.*' He smiled reassuringly. 'Tuesday. It is all arranged. Charles will ring you and tell you what time to be at the airport.'

'All right, thank you. Sorry to fuss.'

'No problem.' With a last wave he turned away, back to his aircraft, and she went on out, where, hopefully, her mother was waiting with the car.

She enjoyed the long weekend, seeing Nita, her other friends, showing off the baby, but when Tuesday came and went with no call from Charles she began to feel frightened. Hadn't she told herself he wouldn't come back for her? From fear she went to bleak misery, and then to panic. Supposing he'd had an accident? But then Jean-Marc would have called. Supposing they'd both had an accident?

Every five minutes she tried ringing the house, but there was never any answer. In desperation she rang the casino, only to be met with evasive answers to her many questions. Where was Charles? Jean-Marc? She tried ringing the airport, asked for Jacques. 'No, sorry, Jacques isn't here.'

By Wednesday evening panic had turned to certainty that something was wrong. She tried to book herself a flight from Gatwick, Heathrow, anywhere, but there were no flights into St Gatien in the winter. Only private charters. 'Can you put me through to the charters?' 'No, sorry, there's no one there at the moment.'

Slamming down the phone, she announced stormily, 'Right. I'll get a ferry!'

'For goodness' sake, Melly, be sensible! He's probably just away; he'll ring just as soon as he gets back,' her mother exclaimed impatiently.

'Gets back from where?' she demanded fretfully.

'Well, I don't know, do I? Anyone would think you didn't like staying with us!'

'Oh, don't be silly, of course I do! I'm just worried about Charles!'

'No need to worry about that one!' With a little sniff she went back into the kitchen.

'What was that for?' Melly demanded.

'What was what for?'

'Mother! Don't be aggravating! The little sniff you gave! I know you don't like him——'

'I never said that...'

'You didn't have to! You make it perfectly obvious! Won't come out on your own unless Daddy can bring you! Won't hold a civilised conversation with him!'

'I have always been polite, Melissa!'

'I didn't say you hadn't! But you don't like him. I know you don't!'

'It's not a question of like. If you love him——'

'You know I do!'

'Then there's nothing more to be said.' Stirring the stew with a violence it didn't deserve, or need, she muttered, 'I just don't trust him. Never have, never will. He has too much charm. And just look at the way he treats his poor parents.'

Well, there was no arguing with that, she thought defeatedly. But there had to be a reason for him never talking about them, never going to visit. But where was he? Refusing to give up, she went back to the hall and dialled International Enquiries. Victoire might know.

'Hello? *Est-ce que je peux parler à Victoire, s'il vous plaît*?'

'*Un instant.*'

'*Bonsoir*?'

'Victoire? It's me, Melly. Yes, yes, I'm fine, and the baby—Victoire,' she broke in desperately, 'do you know where Charles is? Or Jean-Marc? I can't seem to get hold of them! Hello? Victoire? Are you still there?'

'Yes, of course, sorry; I was just asking Sebastien, but he doesn't know either. We haven't seen them for several days. Do you want me to try and find out?'

'Oh, please,' she said gratefully. 'I've been worried sick. Jacques was supposed to pick me up yesterday.'

'Oh, well, OK, don't worry; give me your number, and I'll ring you back. It might not be until tomorrow.'

'That's all right, I just didn't know who else to ask.'

'No problem, and please don't worry. I'm sure everything's fine.'

'Yes,' she agreed without conviction.

An hour later the phone rang. Snatching it up, she said breathlessly, 'Victoire?'

'No, it's me. Charles.'

'Charles! Where the devil have you been? I've been worried sick! No one seemed to know where you were, and——'

'Hold on, hold on,' he broke in, 'what on earth are you talking about? You know where I was——'

'No, I don't! You said I was to be picked up yesterday——'

'Melly!' he interrupted. 'Didn't David ring you?'

'David? No.'

'Are you sure?'

'Well, of course I'm sure!' she exclaimed crossly. 'Do you think I——?'

'All right, all right,' he broke in soothingly, 'I'm sorry, it's just that I asked David to ring you and tell you that Jacques couldn't get over yesterday, that you weren't to worry, and that I would ring you today.'

'Oh. Well, he didn't!' she retorted petulantly.

'No, so I gather. Oh, hell, the last thing I wanted was for you to be worried or upset. Damn David.'

'But why didn't you ring me yourself?' she asked, puzzled.

'Because—because, well, I was tied up in a business meeting——Jean-Marc!' he suddenly yelled. 'Will you stop making that bloody racket? I can't hear myself think! Right,' he continued more calmly, 'sorry about that. Look, I'll explain it all later, when I see you.'

'When will that be?'

'Er—I'm not quite sure.'

Hardly comforted by his evasive tone, she frowned. And what the devil was Jean-Marc doing that necessitated making all that noise she could still hear going on in the background? Wanting only to get home and find out for herself, she asked hopefully, 'Shall I come over on the ferry?'

'No! No, you're to wait for Jacques. Look, why don't you stay another week? Hm? I'm a bit busy at the moment . . .'

Doing what? And why should his being busy prevent her from going home? 'I don't want to stay another week,' she said in a small voice.

'Oh, Melly, don't be difficult,' he pleaded tiredly. 'It's not convenient for you to come back right now. It will spoil everything.'

Convenient? What did that mean? Spoil? Spoil what? Thoroughly bewildered, and not knowing how to insist, she asked unhappily, 'Are you at the house?'

'What? Yes, of course I am.'

'I tried to ring you. Last night and today. There was no answer...' And then she distinctly heard a woman laugh. 'Who's there with you?' she asked suspiciously.

'No one! Well, only Jean-Marc. Why?'

'I thought I heard a woman laugh.'

'Nonsense. Look, I have to go—and you're to stay there until I ring again. You understand?'

'Very well,' she agreed miserably. She could still distinctly hear sounds in the background—it sounded like a party. Was that it? He was making the most of his freedom? Having a high old time before she got back? Supposing he didn't want her back? Supposing he decided that he didn't really want the baby either?

'Melly? Are you still there?'

'Yes.'

'Well, don't sound so depressed,' he said with what sounded suspiciously like a false laugh. 'Everything's going to be fine. I'll ring you Monday about bringing you back. All right?'

'All right,' she agreed, but he'd already gone. Back to his party? Replacing the receiver, she stood staring at it for ages until she heard the baby crying for her feed. Turning miserably away, she went to get her.

It had definitely been a woman's voice, she thought as she sat feeding Lauren. A young woman's voice. And why had Jean-Marc been banging? If it was Jean-Marc. And Charles had sounded irritable, impatient. He never sounded impatient usually, so why was he now? Because he'd been forced to ring her? Had he seen Victoire and she'd told him Melly was looking for him? If she'd been secure in his love she could have asked him. Demanded to be told what was going on. But he didn't love her, and it was beginning to sound as if he didn't want her back. Even more disquieting was the news Victoire had when she rang the next morning.

'Hello, Melly? Good news. I've found him! Or, at least, I know where he is!' she laughed. 'It seems Charles and Jean-Marc took *Wanderer* out and—um—well, they aren't back yet.'

'Aren't back?' she echoed in confusion. 'When did they go?'

'Oh, days since!' she said airily. 'So, no need to worry.'

What the devil was going on? Did Victoire genuinely not know? Or had someone told her what to say? 'Who told you they were out on *Wanderer*?' she asked slowly.

'Told me? Er—Nikko. Yes, I think it was Nikko. I went to the casino and enquired.'

'Last night.'

'Yes.'

'And Charles wasn't there?'

'No. I just said he's out with the boat.'

'Is he? How odd,' she retorted sarcastically, 'then perhaps you can explain how he managed to ring me from the house when he's out with the boat?'

'He rang you?' she asked cautiously. 'When?'

'Last night, not long after I spoke to you.'

'Ah. And he said he was at the house?'

'Yes!'

'Oh—well, perhaps he only pretended to be at the house and was really on the boat but didn't want to worry you.'

'Perhaps. Funny, though, it didn't sound like a ship-to-shore link—you can usually tell.'

'Oh, can you?'

'Yes. What's going on, Victoire?'

'Nothing! What should be going on?'

'I don't know, that's why I asked. Are you sure you didn't see Charles last night? I mean, he didn't tell you to tell me he was out on *Wanderer* so that I wouldn't keep ringing?'

'No! And if he rang you himself that proves it, doesn't it? Look, I have to go; I'll see you when you get back next week! Bye!'

Staring thoughtfully at the phone, she wondered how Victoire knew she was returning next week instead of this, as previously arranged. She hadn't told her. So who had? Charles? It had to have been Charles. All right, she decided, she would give him until Monday. If he didn't ring then, she would go out on the ferry and to hell with his instructions! She needed to know what was going on—and intended to find out! She might not be loved, but she was his wife, and, as such, deserved to know the truth! Even if it wasn't something she wanted to hear.

CHAPTER EIGHT

NEVER had days passed so slowly. Melly couldn't take any interest in anything; barely listened to her mother; smiled only vaguely at her father; and wished away the time. She missed Charles like hell. It was ten times worse now than it had ever been before she had lived with him. She needed him with her. Needed to see him.

Sunday night she barely slept at all.

He didn't ring Monday.

By Tuesday morning she could wait no longer. 'I'm going to France!' she announced baldly.

'Very well,' her mother agreed with a fatalistic shrug. 'I think you're wrong, chasing him; however, as you've pointed out on more than one occasion, it's none of my business. The baby can stay with me...'

'No. Lauren comes too.'

'Don't be ridiculous! You can't drag a baby all over France...'

'I don't intend to. I'll get the ferry to Ouistreham, then the train to Deauville...'

'In the dark?' her mother protested angrily. 'Do you have no sense of responsibility? A tiny baby——'

'Mother!' Melly broke in. 'I'm going!' Relenting slightly, when she realised how genuinely worried her mother was, she said more gently, 'Babies are really very tough, you know. She'll be warmly wrapped up; do you honestly think I would take chances with her?'

'No, of course not, but——'

'No buts. And are you trying to tell me that you never took me out when I was a baby? Never carried me anywhere?'

'Well, no—but I never went junketing off to France!'

'You went to Scotland, though, didn't you?' Melly teased. 'I remember you telling me.'

'That was different . . .'

'Was it? Why?'

Staring at her daughter as though she'd like to smack her, she turned and walked away.

Feeling sad that she and her mother could not be the friends she would like them to be, she hurried upstairs to begin her packing. Remembering her old rucksack, she dragged it out, and pushed everything in. It would be easier to carry the baby if she didn't have to carry a suitcase as well. Slipping her arms into the shoulder straps, she collected the baby's quilted sleeping-bag and went back downstairs.

'And how are you getting to the ferry?' her mother demanded. 'Because, if you think I'm driving you down there, you're mistaken! I don't like driving very far, you know I don't.'

'I don't expect you to,' she said as patiently as she was able. 'I shall get the train.' Carefully fitting Lauren into the warm sleeper and zipping it up, she added, 'I'll ring when I get there, let you know we're OK.' Kissing her mother quickly on the cheek, she left.

Chasing him? No! It was natural to be concerned, wasn't it? To worry about him? That couldn't be called chasing, could it? She just needed to know why. Was he ill? Unable to ring? In which case, why hadn't Jean-Marc let her know? Did he not want them any more? Not want the responsibility, and had made fiction fact by going off in *Wanderer*? Had he been angry that she'd rung Victoire, and was doing this to teach her a lesson? No, Charles was never petty. Then why?

All during that long, tiring trip to France, she asked herself the same questions—and could come up with no satisfactory answers. The journey was a great deal easier than she had expected, for, although there was a lot of waiting about, in ferry terminals, railway stations, people were exceptionally kind when they saw she had a small baby. She was ushered into warm waiting-rooms at railway stations, given a cabin on the ferry, and, although, when she finally arrived in Deauville, at ten minutes past eight the following morning, she was tired, the baby had taken no harm at all. Was, in fact, sleeping peacefully, snug and warm in her sleeping-bag.

More worried than anything else, an ache in her arms and back, she took a taxi to the house. Fitting her key into the lock, she pushed open the door, and then just stared in shock. The house was empty; she could see it was empty. Not just of people, but of everything. Hurrying from room to room, the rucksack still on her back, Lauren still clasped in her arms, she stared at empty rooms. No furniture, no carpets, curtains, nothing. Unable to comprehend what her eyes were telling her, she stood in what had once been Lauren's nursery and shook with fear. Where was he? Where was everything? Hearing a noise downstairs, and a hesitant voice, she hurried out on to the landing. The old lady from the house next door was standing in the hall.

'Madame Fontanel!' Melly called urgently before hurrying down to join her.

'*Madame*?' she queried in surprise. 'What you do here?'

'Looking for Charles,' she whispered in a frightened little voice. 'Where is he?'

'Monsieur Revington?'

'*Oui*. Do you know? Er—*est-ce que vous savez*?'

Giving an infuriating shrug, she shook her head. '*Non*.'

'Melly?'

Spinning round in shock, she stared at Fabienne, and then just stood helplessly by as she ushered the next-door neighbour out and closed the door. Staring at David's wife, her eyes wide, she asked helplessly, 'Where's Charles?'

'Gone.'

'Gone?'

'Yes. Didn't he leave you a message? No, obviously not,' she answered herself, 'else you wouldn't be here.'

'But where has he gone?'

With a shrug every bit as infuriating as the one Melly's neighbour had given, she said, 'I do not know. No one does. He just went. Put everything in store, put the house up for sale, and went.'

'He wouldn't leave without telling me. He wouldn't leave without the baby!'

'Oh, don't be so naïve! She was a novelty! Do you really think a man like Charles would want to tie himself down with a baby?'

'He loves her!'

'Of course he does! She's his daughter! But that doesn't mean he wants to see her, hear her screaming, twenty-four hours a day! The poor man's been exhausted! He could hardly wait to pack you off to your mother, now, could he? Look, I know we've had our differences, but what would I have to gain by lying to you? Here, give me the baby; you look exhausted!'

Numb and bewildered, she handed Lauren over.

'It really was naughty of him just to light out without a word to you. He might have known you'd come over to see what was going on!' she exclaimed. 'Really, the man is a wretch.'

Slipping her arms out of her rucksack, Melly allowed it to slide to the floor. Leaning back against the wall, rubbing her sore arms, she continued to stare at Fabienne. She'd been barely listening to her because her mind had still been searching down every avenue to find a reason, but when Fabienne continued to paint a black picture she snapped irritably, 'Oh, stop it! Charles wouldn't do that!'

'Oh, my poor innocent,' she sighed, and she sounded so sympathetic, so kind, that for a moment Melly found herself actually considering her words. 'I've known him a long time,' she continued, 'ever since he's lived here, and, much as I like him, much as everyone does, we all know—well, we all know why he got married,' she finished in a little rush. 'Oh, he never discussed it, of course not, Charles never does, but, well, he *liked* being a bachelor.

Liked to be free to do whatever it was he wanted to do. He is a man of great complexity, and quite ruthless when there is the need. I know he likes to give the impression of only being witty and charming, but you surely must know that is not the true picture. He also, I think, gets bored easily. Why else does he begin so many ventures? It cannot only be to make money. Well, in my opinion, marriage was a venture, and he eventually got bored. I expect he will come to visit you from time to time. He'll probably feel guilty for a bit, embarrassed, probably turn up and expect you to understand, but he's not a man for taming, Melly, you know that. Look how he went off power-boat racing when you were about to have the baby.'

'That was because....' Unable to explain, or not wanting to explain, she looked away.

'Ring David if you don't believe me,' she persisted, 'he'll tell you; I expect the phone's still connected. Oh, I know what you're going to say,' she insisted, despite the fact that Melly hadn't been going to say anything, 'that David is hardly a reliable person to ask after failing to ring you last week. But that was *not* his fault! It was mine. He could not get through, so he asked me to do it! Well, I forgot!' she said defiantly. 'I am very sorry.'

Staring at the other woman, feeling weary and shell-shocked, and not believing for a moment that her memory had been at fault but that it had been a piece of deliberate meddling, she watched her bend to pick up the phone from the floor.

Listening for a moment to be sure she had a dial tone, Fabienne punched out her home number. 'David? Yes, it's me.' There was a little pause while presumably David answered, and then Fabienne rushed on quickly, 'Look, the most awful thing has happened. Melly's here! Yes, she just turned up—no, apparently he didn't let her know or anything.' There was another little pause, and then she continued, 'Will you tell Melly that you don't know where he is? She doesn't believe me, I'm afraid. All right, hold on.' With a wry little grimace, she passed the phone across, and, hoisting the baby into a more comfortable position, she waited.

'Hello?' Melly said hesitantly.

'Hi, Melly. Still looking for Charles? Well, I'm really sorry, but Fabienne is right, no one knows where he is. I shouldn't worry about it; I expect he'll turn up—he usually does. Look, I have to go; I'll see you later, I expect.' And, with that, he put the phone down. Frowning at the buzzing receiver, she slowly replaced it. Even for David, that had been rather abrupt. Had he been embarrassed? He'd sounded...well, he'd sounded the way Victoire had sounded, a sort of 'oh, my God, it's Melly, what the hell do we tell her?' Straightening, she looked at Fabienne.

'I'm sorry, Melly, I really am. I know you don't like me—and, to be honest, I never liked you very much, but I wouldn't have wished this on you. Go home, that's the best thing, and, as David said, wait till he contacts you. Because he will, in a few days, a week. Come on, I'll run you back to the ferry terminal.'

Stubbornly shaking her head, frantically trying to think, she said, 'I'll try the casino...'

'At eight-thirty in the morning? Oh, Melly, there won't be anyone there!'

Automatically accepting the baby back, she asked slowly, 'How did you know I was here?'

'Well, you don't need to sound so suspicious! I'd just dropped a friend at the station when I saw you come out. I knew you must be coming to the house. I hooted to attract your attention, and then got boxed in by another car. By the time I'd got free you'd gone, so I drove straight here.'

'Oh.' Feeling empty and destroyed, she continued to stare blankly at the other woman. Who else could she try? Victoire? But Victoire had lied; why should she expect her to tell the truth now? And Fabienne was right, they were all Charles's friends, not hers, not really, only by association, and David wouldn't have lied...

'I truly wish I could tell you different,' Fabienne said softly, 'but I can't. You could come and stay with us...' she added with a rather dubious air.

Shaking her head, Melly tried to think what she should do. Go back to Beckford and hope that he would contact her? But it seemed so tame to go back when she had come all this way. But supposing she did find him? And he didn't want her? Suppose there was a scene? No, she couldn't cope with that.

'Come on,' Fabienne encouraged again, 'my car's outside. I'll carry the rucksack.'

'Did he go in *Wanderer*, did you say?' Melly asked listlessly.

'Yes, with Jean-Marc.'

Feeling frozen, and empty, and, even though she had been half expecting that he wouldn't want her back, disbelieving, she finally allowed Fabienne to run her back to Ouistreham.

By eight o'clock that evening she was back in Beckford. Her mother, thankfully, had the sense to keep quiet. Her father was out, at his bowls club. Slumping in the armchair, the baby still cradled in her lap, she stared at the wall.

When the gods started to be malicious they didn't let go; not half an hour after she had arrived home there was a knock at the door. Melly was vaguely aware of raised voices, arguments, and then the lounge door opened and Charles's parents stood there. Glancing at them, too tired and hurt to even feel surprised, she nevertheless tightened her hold on Lauren. The way things were going, she wouldn't have been at all astonished to learn that they had come for the baby.

They looked smug. That was the only word she could think of to describe them. Smug and self-satisfied. She had never liked them, had had as little to do with them as possible over the years; not that they had ever wanted anything to do with her. Before her marriage they had merely nodded to her if they met her in the street. After, they had cut her dead. They had never, as far as she knew, enquired after the baby, and now here they were. Why?

'Your mother rang to ask whether by chance we might know where Charles might be when you returned to France,' Mrs Revington explained with a smile that Melly found repellent. 'We saw you return. He's left you, hasn't he?' she added. She sounded glad.

'No,' Melly denied automatically.

'He's a waster, my dear, a thief. Uncaring of anyone but himself. He has no morals; no sense of responsibility. Although perhaps we, too, have failed in that respect.' She sighed. 'We should have warned you, tried to prevent this. He has bad blood, I'm afraid.' And, whether by accident or design, she glanced at the baby.

'Your blood,' Melly murmured.

'No. Not mine, his mother's,' she said sorrowfully.

Frowning, she queried slowly, 'He's not your son?'

'No, had he been, perhaps things would have turned out differently.' Nodding at the silent man by her side, she added, 'She was Bertram's sister, always wild, always in trouble. She chased a man for his wealth...' 'Just like you' hung in the air, unspoken. But thought, Melly knew, most definitely thought. She might clothe her warnings in a pleasant smile, but the smile cloaked the mind of a zealot. Glancing at Bertram, she saw the same light of conviction in his eyes, and she began to understand a little of what had made Charles the way he was. Had he countered their moralising with smiles of his own? A bland refusal to be cowed?

'The man did not want her,' she continued, 'merely took what was offered, and then discarded her. She came crawling home to us. We took her in for the child's sake——'

'Where is she now?' Melly interrupted.

'Dead.'

She sounded as though it were no more than she deserved, to be dead. 'How did she die?' Melly persisted.

'Quietly, in shame.'

'Oh, don't be so theatrical!' she retorted, infuriated by the pair of them. 'Why did you come here tonight? To gloat?'

'No, in Christian charity. You will need help, support, without a father for your child...'

'The child has a father,' Mrs Morland put in coldly, 'and grandparents, and I did not tell you in order to have you sermonise over my daughter! I rang to ask if you knew where he might be! It was very kind of you to come,' she tacked on lamely, 'but Melly is tired...'

'He won't come back,' Mrs Revington said maliciously. 'Or, if he does, it won't be to see you. He's no good——'

'He has more good in his little finger than either of you has in your whole body!' Melly retorted. 'Whatever he is, whatever he has done, whatever pain he has suffered, can be laid at your door!'

'He lies, he cheats——'

'No. He does neither, and it astonishes me that he could turn out so normal, so charming, after a lifetime of sermonising from the pair of you! Now, if you will excuse me, I'm tired.' She had been going to add that if they wanted to see their grandchild from time to time she would not object, but remembered just in time that they weren't Lauren's grandparents, for which she could only be thankful. 'Goodnight,' she added firmly.

'If you can't see evil where evil exists, then I pity you,' Mrs Revington said self-righteously. 'We gave him everything a child could want. A home, good food, a decent upbringing, and he threw it back in our faces!'

'Did you give him love?' Melly asked wearily. Yet she had given him love, and that hadn't been enough either.

They didn't answer, which was probably just as well, just turned and opened the door—and came face to face with Charles. Brushing past him with barely a glance, they walked along the hall, and Melly heard the front door close behind them.

Her eyes still on Charles, she stared at him. Drank in the sight of him, then frowned in concern when she noticed the large graze on his forehead, the purpling bruise on his temple. When he slumped against the door frame and briefly closed his eyes she half rose from the chair.

'Charles!' she exclaimed in fright. 'What's wrong?'

With what looked like an enormous effort he straightened and opened his eyes. 'I thought... I—— Oh, God, I'm shaking like a leaf. Sorry.'

'Charles?' Mrs Morland exclaimed as she edged past him into the room. 'Oh, good grief, man, you look like death! Whatever is the matter?'

With an odd, shaky little laugh, he said, 'I thought they were dead.'

When both women looked at him in astonishment he explained lamely, 'You obviously haven't seen the news. There was a rail crash, a bad one. The Portsmouth train, and I thought... had convinced myself...' Taking another deep breath, he continued, 'I heard it on the car radio, driving here from the airport, a derailment, many dead, and it was about the time that I thought Melly would have been on the train. Sorry,' he apologised again.

'Oh, my God!' Mrs Morland exclaimed weakly. 'Oh, my God. It could have been ... Oh, heavens.' Collapsing weakly on to the sofa, she continued to stare at Charles with shocked eyes.

'It must have been the train after mine,' Melly said quietly, her own eyes wide with the horror of what might have been. 'If I hadn't run to catch the train I did ... Those poor people.'

'A cup of tea!' Mrs Morland exclaimed. 'That's what we need. Charles, sit down, rest.'

With a lame smile for Melly he did as he was told. 'Sorry,' he apologised again. 'I'm all right now.'

He didn't look all right, he looked grey.

'Baby asleep?' he asked with the obvious desire to change the subject.

Glancing down at Lauren, still curled on her lap, she nodded. Flicking her eyes back to Charles, she asked quietly, 'What happened to your head?'

'What? Oh, something fell on me.' Putting a hand up to touch the graze, almost as if to assure himself that it was still there, he shrugged. 'It's all right, only a graze.'

'It looks sore,' she commented lamely.

'No, I'd forgotten all about it.'

And then it seemed that neither of them knew what to say next. He didn't mention his parents. No, not his parents, she thought with a jolt of surprise, his aunt and uncle, but, as he hadn't so far referred to their visit, she didn't know how to.

'May I hold her?' he asked suddenly.

'Yes, of course,' she agreed, surprised by the hesitant note in his voice. Almost as if he'd thought

she might not want him to. Carefully picking her
up, she passed her to him.

Holding her in the crook of his arm, he smiled
down at her, a genuine smile, quite obviously delighted to see her. Without looking at Melly, he
asked, 'Will it take you long to get ready?'

'Ready?'

'Mm, to leave. Go back to Deauville.'

'I already went——'

'I know.' Raising his eyes to hers, he added
tightly, 'I saw Fabienne. My God! When I think
of you dragging a small baby back and forth on
the ferry, I...' Breaking off, his jaw clenched, he
shook his head as though he couldn't put into words
what he was feeling.

'She was all right,' she whispered. His words had
made her feel guilty, and ashamed, and yet she had
no reason to; the baby had been in no danger. 'She
was well wrapped up,' she added. Was he angry
because he thought she had put his daughter at risk?
Or because he hadn't intended to come and see her,
and now felt duty-bound to? And yet he seemed
genuinely pleased to see his daughter. Had been grey
with fear that they, or she, might have been killed.

'I only have a two-hour turn-round...' he began
again, more quietly.

'You're never going now?' Mrs Morland exclaimed. 'You've only just arrived!'

'Yes, I know. Sorry.'

'He only has a two-hour turn-round,' Melly explained with some bewilderment.

'But it's dark!'

'Yes,' he agreed with a tired smile, then, glancing briefly at his watch, he added, 'I have to take off in an hour's time.'

Still staring at him, trying to read his face, she began hesitantly, 'The house was empty...'

'Yes, I'll explain later. Go and pack. Please.'

Nodding, glancing at her mother to see the same look of bewilderment that she was no doubt wearing, she got up and walked to the door. To her further surprise, Charles followed her upstairs to her room. Perching on the edge of her bed, his eyes on his daughter, he still seemed distracted, exhausted, and, feeling rather dazed and bewildered herself, she just stood there and continued to stare at him. 'They aren't your parents,' she said stupidly.

'No. No questions, Melly, not now, I don't think I could cope with them. Anyway, there's no time. We'll talk later.'

'You really want me to come?'

Flicking his eyes up to hers, he said carefully, 'Yes, Melly, I really want you to come.'

With a little nod, she began to pack.

'Did you have a good visit?' he asked in a rather strained voice.

'Sure,' she replied with a bitter little smile. 'Terrific. I went to France and came back. Saw some old friends, did some shopping.' Got bored, she added mentally. Frustrated, lonely, afraid. The sad truth was that, apart from missing Charles, being afraid that he didn't want her back, she'd grown out of Beckford. Without quite realising it, she'd changed. And people she had known, and liked, all her life had changed towards her. The remarks that were made about her expensive clothes, the expert cutting of her hair, weren't admiring, or teasing, but had an edge to them. Jealousy? she wondered. Envy? Or just plain cattiness? A small town with small minds. No, that wasn't entirely fair; partly it was her own fault because she had refused to answer questions about Charles. They might all put him down, call him a no-good, but they had all been eager for any gossip about him. Jealous of his wealth, his business acumen, his lifestyle. And him? What had he really been up to? Why had he come back?

Unable to leave the subject alone, she persisted, 'Why didn't you come?'

'Oh, Melly, not now. Please not now.'

'All right,' she agreed distantly. 'How's Jean-Marc?'

'He's fine.'

'And Victoire?' she couldn't resist asking. 'Seen anything of her and Sebastien?'

When he didn't immediately answer she looked at him sharply. He was staring at her with a rather odd expression on his face; half chagrined, half amused. 'Yes, I saw Victoire. Get on with your packing.'

Taking the last two dresses from the wardrobe, she carefully folded them and laid them on top of the case.

'Is that the lot?' he queried, and when she nodded he got to his feet. 'Right, let's go.'

'Is Jacques waiting at the airport?'

'No, I flew over myself. Here, you take the baby, I'll carry the bags.'

Taking Lauren, she led the way downstairs. Walking into the lounge, she gave her mother a wan smile. 'I'll ring you. Say goodbye to Dad for me.' Giving her an awkward kiss on the cheek, she added softly, 'Take care. And thank you for trying to find him.'

With a rather sad, rueful smile, and looking more than a little embarrassed, Mrs Morland murmured, 'Opened a can of worms there, didn't I? And, Melly,' she added in a rush, 'I'm sorry if I've been less than gracious to Charles.' Looking away for a moment, she took a deep breath before blurting out, 'I was jealous. I'd lost Donny, and it felt as though I was losing you!'

'Oh, Mum!' she exclaimed helplessly. Giving her an awkward hug, she said gently, 'You can come any time, you know that.'

'Yes. Tell Charles I'm sorry.'

'Why not tell him yourself?'

Shaking her head, she gave her daughter a push towards the door. 'Go on, off you go; give me a ring when you get there—home,' she substituted. 'And if you need me, well, you know where I am.'

'Yes.'

Feeling tearful and exhausted, she went out to join Charles in the hire-car.

It was a little after half-past eleven when they landed at St Gatien, and, handing the plane over to the mechanics, Charles led the way to where he had left his car. A cold wind was blowing off the sea, and she shivered as he helped her into the back seat. Handing her the baby, he put the luggage in the boot and climbed behind the wheel.

At first she didn't notice anything different, just lay back, thinking her own thoughts, worrying. She had no idea where they were going—a hotel, she supposed—but when they turned right at the traffic-lights, away from the town, she frowned and stared intently from the window. 'Where exactly are we going?'

'You'll see,' he replied quietly.

With a tired little sigh she leaned back again. She felt as though she had been travelling forever; that she would never again lie in her own bed, sleep. Yet, unbelievably, she was back in France, back with him; surely anything else could be worried about later?

When he slowed the car, and turned in between high gates, she stared at the large, dark house at the end of the drive with a frown of surprise. It was the house that had always intrigued her. On the opposite side of Deauville to their old house, she had often seen it when she'd been going to Lisieux. It stood in about two acres of land, wild, overgrown, interesting, and she had often longed to go in and explore. Except you couldn't very well go into someone else's house without an invitation! But Charles hadn't known who lived here either, he'd said so when she'd asked, so why was he coming here now?

When he brought the car to a halt she looked up at the odd little veranda that ran round the top storey, at the funny-shaped windows. The whole place looked both secretive and inviting, a sort of gingerbread house.

With a long, weary sigh he switched off the engine and leaned back. 'I had a plan,' he said softly, 'and every damned thing that could go wrong with it did.' Turning to face her, he continued, 'Melly, I'm sorry you were worried, frightened . . .' With another sigh he gave an odd little laugh. 'Come on, let's get you inside; you must be exhausted. We can talk later.'

'But who lives here?' she exclaimed. 'It doesn't even look as though they're still up! Are you sure they won't mind us turning up like this?'

'No, Melly, they won't mind at all.' Helping her out, he kept hold of her arm in case she stumbled in the dark. 'Baby not too heavy?'

'No, she's fine.'

To her continuing surprise, he took a key from his pocket, but before he could fit it in the lock the door was swung open and the porch light switched on. A young woman stood there. She was laughing.

'Oh, God!' he exclaimed. 'What are you doing here?'

'Waiting for you, of course!' Bending forward, she kissed him on both cheeks. 'Welcome home! And you must be Melly!' she added with a broad grin. Holding the door wide, she ushered them inside.

Bewildered and not a little suspicious, Melly allowed herself to be hustled towards a door along the passage on the left. Looking from Charles, who looked defeated, to the unknown woman, she waited. With a barely suppressed smile, the woman threw open the door.

The room seemed full of people, all laughing, and Charles groaned again, then winced when they shouted in unison, 'Surprise!'

With a violent start the baby woke up and began to scream. Pandemonium reigning, someone removed Lauren from her hold; someone else pressed a glass into her hand; people kissed her, hugged her, and all seemed to talk at once. Her face registering her utter confusion, she gradually sorted out the faces. Victoire and Sebastien, Nikko with his arm round the young woman who had opened the door—in fact, practically everyone she knew in Deauville. Including David, but without Fabienne, or, at least, not as far as she could see.

'Welcome back,' Jean-Marc said from beside her. He sounded pleased.

Turning her bewildered gaze on him, she whispered, 'But what is all this for? And whose house is it?'

With a gentle smile, he said softly, 'Yours.'

'Mine? But how can it be?'

'Because,' he continued with a great deal of amusement, 'Charles had this really great idea! He's had me working like a slave!'

'Don't exaggerate . . .'

'But I don't understand,' she insisted, ignoring Charles's interruption. Or didn't want to understand? she wondered. Did Jean-Marc mean this was to be her house alone, that Charles had bought it for her and was now going off wherever he had been going before?

'Don't you like it?' he queried with a crooked smile.

'Yes. No. Oh, I don't know!'

'Well, you'd better,' he warned, 'because I absolutely refuse to move everything back again!'

Pushing up the arm of his jacket, he showed her a long gouge in his forearm. 'Look!' he exclaimed dramatically. 'Walking wounded! We were *both* wounded in one way or another!'

Turning back to Charles, she stared at the graze on his forehead.

'Mm.' With a wry look, he confessed, 'A tile fell on me.'

'From the roof?'

'From the roof,' he confirmed solemnly.

'That's what you were doing when you rang me?'

'Yes, that's why you couldn't come back. It all took much longer than expected to get the place straight. As Jean-Marc said, we've been working like slaves!'

'But you surely didn't do it all yourselves!'

'Good heavens, no!' he exclaimed, looking so astonished that she gave a faint smile. 'I hired a firm to do it.'

'Then what on earth were you and Jean-Marc doing to get wounded?'

Looking slightly sheepish, he admitted, 'We helped.'

'Interfered,' Jean-Marc put in softly. 'Charles didn't think they could get it absolutely right without his invaluable assistance,' he added drily.

'Overseeing,' Charles corrected. 'Organising them more effectively.'

It didn't sound like Charles; whenever he wanted something done, he always employed the best. And if they were the best, why on earth had they needed overseeing?

As though understanding her thoughts, Jean-Marc whispered, 'It was too important to be left to others. It had to be exactly right.'

'But you helped too,' she accused in some perplexity. 'When Charles rang me you were banging.'

'*Non*,' he denied, 'the carpenters. But he could hardly tell them to stop when you weren't to know they were here, could he?'

'And he only got the scratch,' Charles put in, 'because he was trying to get his beloved kitchen straight before the decorators had finished.'

'But who did the house belong to? I don't remember that it was up for sale.'

'It wasn't then, but as soon as I heard that it was I put in a bid. It was finalised the day I packed you off to your mother's, then had the devil's own job finding a builder that was free straight away.'

'But why?' she asked, still confused. 'You'd only just done the other house up when I had Lauren.'

'We decided it was too small. We needed land—for a pony,' he explained as though she should immediately understand. 'Lauren will want a pony.'

'She will?'

'Of course.'

And who was this 'we' he kept talking about? 'And was that why you didn't come to collect me on Monday? Because it still wasn't finished?'

Glancing at Jean-Marc, and then at David, who had come to join them, he shook his head. 'No. That was another reason.'

'What other reason?' she demanded with a little bubble of hysteria. 'What? That you hadn't been intending to come at all? That this elaborate arrangement, this house, was to be a sop to your conscience? You were going to leave, weren't you? And not tell me at all?'

The sudden, shocked silence in the room was the last straw. With a little sob she whirled and ran out.

CHAPTER NINE

'No! MELLY, no,' Charles said more gently. Catching her arm, he turned her against him, and held her in the circle of his arms. Jean-Marc carefully closed the door on the revellers and joined them in the hall. Five seconds later David slipped out.

'He was in the hospital,' Jean-Marc said quietly. 'Unconscious. The builders were fixing some loose tiles on the roof; one fell off and hit him where he stood below watching. I didn't know that he'd promised to ring and come for you on Monday. He hadn't told me.'

'Hospital?' she repeated weakly. 'Unconscious?' Staring up at Charles, as if to make sure that he was really all right, she glanced back to Jean-Marc. 'But why didn't you let me know?'

'Because I didn't want to worry you.'

'And Fabienne didn't know? She didn't say anything about ... She said all those things about you not wanting me. I've been going out of my mind.'

'Oh, Melly,' David put in. 'I'm so sorry, it's all my fault. When I spoke to you—you see, Charles had made us promise not to tell you about the house, it was to be a surprise, and when Fabienne rang I was in such a panic not to say the wrong thing, blurt it out, that I didn't stop to think until afterwards. That was when I realised you must be in France. It stupidly never occurred to me when

162

Fabienne rang; I thought you were in England. It was only later that I realised my mistake, because I knew Fabienne wasn't in England...' Looking muddled and confused, then cross with himself for being so inarticulate, he gave her a look of helplessness.

'But she told you, I heard her!' Melly insisted tearfully.

'No.' He frowned. 'All she said was, tell Melly you don't know where Charles is. So I did.'

Shaking her head, tired, confused and unhappy, she argued, 'No. She said...she said—oh, I don't know, I can't remember, but she definitely told you I was there, at the house! She said Charles had gone away, that he didn't want the responsibility of me and the baby; that she didn't know where he was and, if I didn't believe her, to ask you!'

'No,' he denied. Staring worriedly at her, he shook his head. 'No, she wouldn't do that... I know she didn't ring you before when she was supposed to, but she really wouldn't have lied to you. Look, the phone rang,' he explained, 'I picked it up, and she said, "It's me," and I said, "Hang on a minute while I turn the radio off," because it was difficult to hear what she was saying. I put the phone down, walked across and turned off the radio, then I came back, and she said, "Tell Melly you don't know where Charles is." So I did,' he repeated, 'because I didn't. I mean, I didn't know he was in the hospital!'

'And while you were away from the phone,' Jean-Marc said softly, 'isn't it possible that your dear wife said all the things Melly said she said, but with no one to hear them but Melly?'

'No,' David denied weakly, 'she wouldn't do that. Or, at least, she might have said something to make Melly go back to England because she didn't know what else to say without letting the secret out. Yes, that must be it; she took you back to the port because she didn't know where else to take you—and I expect you misunderstood what she said,' he concluded lamely, but he didn't seem very convinced by his explanation. Neither did anyone else.

With none of them quite knowing what to say next, it was finally Charles who broke the deadlock. Glancing at Jean-Marc over her head, he instructed softly, 'Get rid of them all, will you? Thank them for coming, tell them we'll have a proper house-warming later.'

'Yes. And you and Melly had better have a long talk, I think. Come on, David.' Taking the other man's arm, he urged him back towards the lounge.

'Come on, Melly,' Charles insisted quietly. 'We'll go upstairs, where we can talk in peace.'

'What about the baby?'

'Jean-Marc will look after her. Come on.' His arm still round her shoulders, he led her up the oddly crooked staircase to the landing. Opening the door at the end, he stood back for her to enter.

The nursery—and she had an overwhelming feeling of *déjà vu*. It was exactly the same as in the other house. A little larger, maybe, but everything else was an exact replica. The curtains, carpet, wallpaper. 'It's the same,' she whispered dazedly.

A rather forced note in his voice, he exclaimed, 'Of course it is! Lauren's only just got used to the other one; we don't want her getting confused, now, do we?'

'No,' she agreed. With a shuddery little sniff she stared round her with tear-washed eyes.

Taking her hand, he led her to the door in the corner. Pushing it open, he tugged her inside. 'Your room,' he said quietly.

That, too, was the same. Barely able to comprehend anything, she walked across the room and sat on the edge of the bed—just as she had before. It didn't make any sense. The other house had been plenty big enough; and it had been she who had liked this house, not him, and he couldn't have bought it for her benefit! He just couldn't have! 'Why?' she asked helplessly.

With a funny little smile that she, had she not known him better, would have thought embarrassed, he closed the door to the nursery and leaned back against it. 'You always liked it——'

'Oh, Charles,' she broke in, 'I don't think I can take much more. Please don't play games! You don't like me. Don't trust me, so don't tell me you went to all this expense just for me, because that really is a horse that won't run!' Her voice breaking, she swallowed hard before resuming. 'Now tell me the real reason.'

Looking down for a moment, he crossed one ankle over the other and shoved his hands into his pockets. 'I don't dislike you . . .'

'Charles! Stop prevaricating! Why?'

'Inducement,' he admitted quietly.

'Inducement for what?'

Raising his head, he stared at her. His steady grey eyes searching hers, he finally said, 'For you to stay.'

'But I would have stayed!' she exclaimed in bewilderment.

'Would you? After the way I behaved I thought you would hate me.'

'Of course I don't hate you,' she whispered in perplexity.

'Then in that case...' Taking a deep breath, he continued awkwardly, 'I need to ask you something, and I don't quite know how to do it.'

With a horrible feeling that she knew exactly what was coming, she clenched her hands into fists before instructing thickly, 'Just ask.'

'All right. Do you still love me?' he asked bluntly.

'What?' she asked blankly.

'Melly!'

Wrenching her gaze from his, she stared at the cot. 'Why do you want to know?'

With seeming irrelevance he explained, 'I tried to ask you before, after Lauren was born, and since, but there never seemed to be time on our own. You were either preoccupied with the baby, tired, asleep, or there were other people there. Ever since I found out about your—"obsession", it's been going round and round in my head. I couldn't understand, believe, how ordinary, nice people could feel like that. Until I got the message to say that you were having the baby. When I rang the hospital, spoke to the doctor, he scared the hell out of me, Melly.' His eyes losing focus as he remembered that day, he continued quietly, 'He said he feared the baby was becoming stressed, that your health was suffering. Your blood-pressure was erratic, you were tired and listless, too pale; the baby was still breech, and they were worried. For a doctor to say he's worried...'

Swallowing hard, he resumed, 'Anyway, they were whisking you off to surgery, he said, and suggested I get there as soon as I could. I arrived five minutes after they'd wheeled you in. I paced up and down that damned corridor, feeling helpless and useless and frightened. Unable to do anything. I wanted to be in there with you, hold your hand, anything! And I remembered what you had said about loving. About wanting, needing, to do whatever you could; just to be near... And I was so terrified that I would lose you. When a buzzer sounded and two doctors came haring up the corridor and rushed into the operating theatre, I was convinced that it had all gone horribly wrong. Then, after what seemed like hours, the doors opened and they wheeled you out. A nurse was walking beside the trolley, carrying the baby. She put her into my arms and said, "Congratulations, you have a lovely little daughter." Oh, Melly,' he confessed softly, 'I can't explain how I felt. I had never been able to imagine feeling like that, was so sure I never could. I love that baby. More than I could ever have imagined possible! And when I look at her, hold her, I get such an overwhelming feeling of love that it frightens me. Suppose anything happened to her? I couldn't bear it, Melly. And when she cries, and I don't know why, I understand about feeling helpless, about wanting to comfort.' Dragging in a long, ragged breath, he continued determinedly, 'What I'm trying to say is that I want the baby to stay here!'

Her face too white, her eyes bruised, she whispered brokenly, 'No. Ah, no. Don't you think I love her too?'

'No!' he exclaimed after a moment's shocked silence. 'Oh, Melly, no!' Hurrying to her, he knelt in front of her. 'I meant you both! Oh, Melly, did you really think I would try to take her away from you?'

'Yes. I thought... You said... In the other house, when you showed me the nursery and the bedroom, you didn't say *my* room, connecting door for *me* to use, and I thought you meant to get a nanny in, send me back to Beckford—or try,' she tacked on, her eyes once more filled with tears.

'No,' he said gently. 'I would not even try. Is that why you came out here when I didn't turn up on the Monday? Because you were afraid I wouldn't come back for you?'

'Yes,' she whispered, 'and afraid that something had happened to you.'

'Oh, God, I'm so sorry. Poor Melly. I missed you, you know...'

'The baby,' she corrected.

'No,' he denied gently, 'both of you. I haven't been very kind to you, have I? I——'

'Yes!' she interrupted fiercely. 'More kind than I had any right to expect!'

With a funny, crooked smile he teased, 'Still my champion, hm?'

'Yes,' she whispered.

'Oh, Melly.' Putting out his hand, he curved his palm against her cheek and rubbed his thumb gently across her chin. Tilting his head to one side, a light of humour in his eyes, he added, 'You don't sound as though you are. Obsessed, I mean. Don't behave as though you are.'

With a faint embarrassed smile she shook her head. 'No. I knew that you would never love me, I've always known that, but just to be near you, be your friend, was more than I had any right to expect. I think I thought that if I kept a low profile, didn't irritate you in any way, it would be all right. So I hid my feelings as best I could.' Glancing once more at him, the faint, rueful smile still in her eyes, she asked, 'Did you fear that I would turn into one of those women you read about in the papers? Hound you? Wreck your car? Attack any woman that came within two feet of you?'

'No, not really,' he denied. 'Mostly I was just confused. I would look at you, tell myself you were the same Melly I had always known, try to convince myself that you hadn't really changed...'

'But you were always waiting for the obsession to show.'

With a little frown in his eyes, he shook his head slightly. 'No, it wasn't really that. It was...well, it was the money.'

'Money?' she asked, puzzled.

Looking slightly ashamed, he explained, 'I didn't entirely believe your story about always having wanted me—or always having wanted me for myself, shall I say? I knew your family were financially stretched, knew you helped them out as much as you could. You'd said yourself that you'd given up work in order to write, and, although you were published, I knew you couldn't be earning much...'

'So you really did think I wanted you for your money,' she said quietly.

'Yes.' Taking her hands in his, he apologised. 'I'm sorry, Melly. It was an awful thing to think, but it hurt me so. I'd been just on the verge of telling you how I felt, wanting our marriage to be a real one...'

'And do you still think it?'

'No! Good God, no! I haven't thought it for a long time. Oh, Melly, what I'm trying to say in my rather ham-fisted fashion is that I would like you both to stay. That if you like—*want*,' he substituted, 'we could perhaps go back to the way we were before Nita told me about you.' Sitting back on his heels, he added earnestly, 'I want to hear her first words, see her take her first steps; I need that very badly, Melly. I don't think I could bear to be just a visiting father, see her only on allotted days. I want her to know I'm her daddy...' With a funny, choked little sound he released her and got to his feet. Walking across to the window, he kept his back to her. 'So what do you think?' he asked huskily. 'Is the house inducement enough?'

'Did you really think I needed an inducement in order to stay?' she asked him quietly.

'I didn't know. I didn't know if anything would work after the way I'd behaved, going off to Monte Carlo like a spoilt little boy and leaving you to cope alone. I felt so guilty. Not a nice feeling, guilt.'

'No,' she agreed, 'it isn't.'

Turning to face her, he gave a faint smile. 'No. Friends again?'

'Friends,' she agreed.

Turning back to the window, he said, 'You can still see over the town from here.'

Getting up and going to join him at the window, she stared out at the lights in the town, and then across to Le Havre on the opposite headland. His nearness, his warmth, was a comfort and a pain. If she moved just slightly her arm would touch his; her head could rest on his shoulder. But if she did that, closed her eyes, she thought she would fall asleep. She felt bone-weary, and, despite the fact that she was no longer worried about him sending her home, she couldn't seem to get the thought into her tired brain. In an attempt to stave off her exhaustion she commented lightly, 'Rather an expensive way to assuage your guilt.'

'Money's not for keeping, Melly,' he said quietly. 'It's for spending, for enjoying. Anyway,' he added with a grin, 'I seem to have rather a lot of it. Fingers in pies, Melly, fingers in pies, and for some odd reason they all got done to a turn.'

'A favourite of the gods,' she agreed.

'So it would seem. I go into ventures for the strangest, sometimes the flimsiest of reasons, or maybe just because it feels right, and they all seem to turn up trumps.'

'Yes,' she agreed again, 'feelings I understand.'

'Yes.' With a friendly smile he put one arm round her shoulders and hugged her to his side. Sweet agony. 'You could have chosen a more worthy subject for your fantasy.'

'Fantasy isn't based on reason,' she denied quietly as she continued to stare out over the town.

'No, seemingly not, else you wouldn't have chosen a gambler.'

'Oh, I don't know. There are worse things to be,' she argued. She quite desperately wanted to snuggle against him, hold him, kiss him, have him kiss her, with passion. Could he hear the accelerated beat of her heart? Feel her racing pulse? Apparently not. With a funny little sigh, and deciding that now was probably as good a time as any to ask something that had been puzzling her, she commanded quietly, 'Tell me about Jean-Marc. Who is he exactly? And don't tell me again that you won him in a poker game.'

With a little chuckle he asked, 'Who told you I didn't?'

'No one. I overheard a conversation once.'

'Ah.' Turning to face her, he smiled. 'He was one of the world's drifters. Rootless, not knowing where he was going, and perhaps not caring. I met up with him one day in the Bahamas. I'd been bumming around the world, trying out *Wanderer*'s paces, and when I slipped into Nassau he was there on the quay. He looked ill, destitute. He offered to crew for me—no, not offered,' he amended with a smile, 'just began crewing. I had no idea who he was, what he was doing there, he never said...'

'And you were too polite to ask...' she smiled.

'Oh, I asked; he just wouldn't say. Something nefarious, I expect,' he commented humorously.

'Jean-Marc? Never!'

'Maybe not, but I suspect there's a great deal more to him than meets the eye. Anyway, presumably because I was feeling in a benevolent mood, I let him get on with it. He's been with me ever since.' With a little chuckle he added, 'And, for some reason he's never explained, he seems to enjoy being a butler.' Silent for a moment while he presumably thought about it, he shook his head and gave another laugh. 'Goodness knows why. After we'd put to sea he became ill, a fever of some sort, so I nursed him, forced aspirins down his throat, cursed him, fed him, did things for him. When he recovered, and without being asked, he did things for me. Crewed, swabbed the deck, cooked. When we made port he'd get the supplies. Put them on my bill,' he added humorously, 'but get them. When I'd had enough of sailing I looked for somewhere to stay for a while, and Deauville turned out to be it. I liked the town, I liked most of the people. I bought a flat at the harbour, and Jean-Marc disappeared for a while. When I bought the house after our wedding he turned up again. And, to be honest, I've got used to having him around. If he left I'd miss him very much.'

'He behaves as though he's the old family retainer,' she commented with a tired grin.

'Yes, and I haven't the faintest idea why. Very clever is Jean-Marc. He knows a great deal about a lot of things. He's also discreet. He irritates the hell out of me sometimes—and sometimes I rely on him too much, and I get the feeling that one day, when I'm not expecting it, he will up sticks and leave, and I'll never hear of him again. Odd.' Lost in his own thoughts, he stared out over the town.

Taking the opportunity to watch him, she shifted slightly so that she could see his face properly. She wanted to trace that classic nose with her finger, press soft kisses to that generous mouth.

'I also owe him a great deal,' he added quietly as though there hadn't been a long silence in between, 'for the way he took care of you when I was away.'

'Yes,' she agreed inadequately, 'but which still doesn't explain why you said you'd won both him and the house in a poker game!'

'No,' he agreed wryly. With a little shrug, he explained, 'Habit, I guess. A desire to keep people guessing. Never let the right hand know what the left's doing—and because it was no one else's business.'

'Not even mine?'

'Ah, that was different. I didn't want you to think I'd gone to any trouble for you. The circumstances of our marriage were difficult enough; and you had seemed reluctant to accept anything, or so I'd thought—sorry,' he apologised quietly.

'You still think I married you for what I could get?'

With a long sigh he shook his head. 'No, but, as I said, that was what hurt me so much. I've always been very fond of you; always been pleased to see you. Strangely I never considered why, just accepted you as part of my past. You weren't like the people here—the women, perhaps I should say—and, as I told you before Nita came, I had come to enjoy being married to you. Yet when she said all those things, and perhaps because most of the women I meet seem to expect, or need, material things, I felt cheated, because I hadn't wanted you to be like that.' With a little frown he continued, almost to himself, it seemed, 'Even the wives of my friends, people I like, seem to expect to be able to buy, or do, anything they want. And their husbands don't seem to find it strange. I'm not saying that their wives don't love them, but the love seems an afterthought, or given because of what they can have. I'm not explaining this very well, but I thought you were different. You always treated me the same, as a friend, as Charles. You didn't stand in awe of me, didn't—fawn! That's one of the things I really hate, being fawned over. Not because they like me, or admire me, but because of my wealth, because of the doors I could open for them, give them entrée into society.'

'Which you never do,' she commented quietly.

'No, but there's always someone who thinks I might. *That's* what I liked about you. You were never in awe of your surroundings. You might not always have wanted to go, but you were never in awe. Just quietly accepted things. Never plagued me for this or that...'

'There's no saying I wouldn't have if circumstances had been different. As it was, I had no right to plague you.'

'N-o, but I don't think you would have anyway. As I said, I enjoyed being married to you; the only thing that did perturb me was your...well, quietness, I suppose. As though you were playing a role.'

'I was,' she put in with quiet honesty.

'Yes, and that's partly why I believed all that Nita said, because I realised then that you had changed. Were being cautious. You didn't get cross, or argue with me, and that in itself should have alerted me earlier. There was always the vague suspicion that things weren't right, but I put it down to the awkwardness of the situation, getting married for perhaps the wrong reasons, or that being pregnant had made you quiet.' Turning to look back over the town, he added softly, 'I was so disappointed in you, Melly. So ready to believe all that I knew in my heart wasn't true. It knocked me off balance—and it made me take a long, hard look at myself.' With a faint, rueful smile he added, 'And I've been going a very long way round in order to tell you something. Something I'd intended to say the night Nita came and spoiled it all.' Pausing, continuing his surveillance of the town, he unexpectedly changed the subject. 'What did you make of the Revingtons? My illustrious aunt and uncle?'

'Revingtons?' she echoed weakly. Taken aback by the abrupt change, and quite desperately wanting to know what it was he had been going to say, she wrenched her mind round to his relatives, and, without even having to consider the matter, pronounced, 'Zealots. Self-righteous. Cold.'

'Obsessed,' he said flatly. 'With morality. It's odd, isn't it, how history sometimes repeats itself? My mother was apparently obsessed by my father. She followed him, had a child by him, was abandoned by him—and then she died. Probably to escape the sermonising by my sainted aunt!'

Was that why he hadn't abandoned her? she wondered with a little shiver. Righting a wrong? 'And your uncle?' she asked faintly. 'Did he sermonise too?'

'Lord, no; not verbal, anyway. No, good old Uncle Bertram preferred the belt.'

'He thrashed you?' she asked, horrified.

'Oh, yes, until I got too big to handle, and then I think he was afraid that I might thrash him.'

'Did you?'

'No. You don't fight fire with fire, Melly; that would have made me no better than him. No, I decided when I was quite young that I would never be as they were. Never! Nothing would ever obsess me to the point that there was a danger of becoming like them.' With a little sigh he resumed, 'I grew up in darkness, Melly. Laughter was forbidden. Joy was forbidden. Innocent pranks got you a thrashing. It was drummed into me day after day after day that my mother was a tramp. A no-good whore. And I used to think, at night, when I lay on my front because my back was too sore, that anything would be preferable to staying in that house. I used to imagine her, as a little girl, growing up in that stifling atmosphere, because presumably her parents were carbon copies of her brother and his wife, and I would cry for her. I never blamed her for running away, for trying to find happiness, but I did blame her for chasing a man who didn't want her. I thought she should have had more pride.'

'Like me.'

'N-o, not exactly, because I hadn't known, until you told me, that I was being chased. I mean, you never made it obvious. You didn't *haunt* me, and I think perhaps my mother did. But, more than that, I blamed Bertram and Edna. If they hadn't made her life so miserable she would never have run away, never chased a man because she needed to be loved.'

'And I didn't have that excuse,' she observed softly, 'so you thought I was only out for what I could get.'

'To my shame, yes, but, although I knew you were loved, it was a stifling kind of love, and I knew your father was in debt—but even then I should have known better than to jump to conclusions. I'm sorry. Are they managing better now? Because, if they do need financial help, you only have to a——'

'No!' she interrupted. Heavens, that would be the last thing she would ever ask him, and thankfully, hopefully, she would never need to. 'The business seems to be picking up now. Whether it was my leaving home, or the baby, or for some other reason, I don't know, but he's actually taking a proper interest in it now. Has taken a younger man in as a partner; seems, at long last, quite enthusiastic. Go on about your aunt and uncle. You blamed them . . .'

'Yes. You're sure they don't need . . .?'

'No,' she said more gently, 'but thank you anyway. Go on.'

'All right. Yes, I blamed them, and I waited. Even as a child, I waited for the years to pass, for me to grow up; and I never, ever let them see what they had done to me. I pretended, Melly. When he thrashed me I would grit my teeth, and smile. When she smashed the treasured collection of model boats I had secretly made I shrugged. But I never forgot, or forgave. And as I got older I would do everything I could to embarrass them, mock them, make them a laughing stock, until they hated me as much as I hated them. I could have left, run away. I chose not to. I chose to create merry hell. In the village; at school; anywhere, in fact, that I could create it. I did not pass exams—didn't sit them half the time—and when I was sixteen I came home one day to find all my possessions on the front path. I left them there and moved in with a school-friend and his mother who lived over the post office.'

'Yes, I remember,' she said softly. 'Your things stayed there a whole week. There was a great deal of speculation about it.'

'Yes. Do you know, I think more goes on in sleepy little villages than ever goes on in big towns?'

'Probably. So you became an adventurer, pretending to care for nobody, wanting nobody to care for you.'

'Pretending?' he queried with a smile.

'Yes,' she said firmly. 'Pretending. Do you really think you can gammon me into thinking otherwise? When I, of all people, have very good reason to know differently? You will never make me believe that your kindness and care after Donny died was pretence.'

With a wry smile he said softly, 'No, of course it wasn't. I cared very much, and you will never know how many times I wanted to go to your parents and tell them to stop hurting you, using you.'

'No, I didn't know. Only knew that you took it on yourself to care for me, and for others, but you didn't care what happened to yourself,' she stated, understanding at last. 'A course of self-destruction.'

Looking thoughtful for a minute, he qualified, 'I don't know that it was so much self-destruction, as a determination to prove I was somebody to be reckoned with. Sin of pride,' he added with a small smile. 'And, to be honest, I enjoyed pitting my wits against others, taking on impossible challenges.'

'And yet, because of the life you had lived—endured—you were the one person to really understand how I felt when Donny died.'

'Yes. You looked so—*haunted*. Were trying to be so brave, so strong, for your parents' sakes, and I admired you for that. You could have been bitter, or angry, and you never were. Just bewildered and hurting. I've always remembered that, and felt close to you because of it, but when I found out about your obsession I was horrified. Shaken. An old chicken come home to roost.'

With a stab of renewed guilt she murmured unhappily, 'I'm sorry.'

'No, don't apologise any more, Melly. If anyone should do so it's me. Because of my hang-ups I readily assumed the worst. Do you know, I think this last year I've gone through more emotions than I ever thought existed? Pleasure, pain, bewilderment, fear—and love. When I flew over to get you, after the fiasco with Fabienne...'

'She did say those things...' she began earnestly.

Smiling down at her, he hugged her to his side. 'I know.'

'She saw me get off the train and followed me to the house...'

'Ssh, it doesn't matter...'

'Yes, it does,' she insisted, 'because I don't understand what she hoped to gain. She must have known that I would tell you what she'd said.'

'I don't think she cared—or perhaps hoped to persuade me that it was you who lied. She told me that you'd said you never wanted to see me again.'

'And did you believe her?'

'I didn't want to believe her, but was half afraid it might be true. And when I think how she made you travel back and forth on that damned ferry!' he finished angrily.

'But Lauren was well wrapped up, quite safe...'

Turning to stare at her in astonishment, he exclaimed, 'No! I wasn't worried about the baby—good lord, I knew you would look after her; no, it was you I was concerned about. It wasn't as if it had been a normal birth; you'd had an *operation*, Melly! It takes ages to get over that! The doctor told me you had to take things easy. That you weren't to be worried. That you might be a bit tearful, depressed, and I'd been doing my damnedest to keep things smooth, easy for you, not bringing up controversial subjects! Why else do you think I've waited so long to tell you how I felt? I packed you off to your mother's when I didn't want to so that you wouldn't have the hassle of moving house. And then the damned thing taking so long! Fabienne sticking her oar in! Victoire making things even worse! And then when I heard about the train crash...! Lord, Melly, I couldn't ever go through that again.'

'But you still haven't told me,' she put in quietly.

'What?'

'You still haven't told me.'

'I haven't?' he asked comically.

'No. Only that you missed me.'

'Yes. Missed seeing you there, missed your smile, missed—— Oh, Melly, I don't know how to explain it. Even with all the misunderstandings between us, you were still a part of me.' With a little shake of his head as though he had no idea how to explain, he resumed, 'So I made the poor builders work like demons to get the house finished quickly so that I could come to fetch you. And then first David didn't ring you when I asked, and you were so upset...'

'Why did you ask David?' she queried, puzzled. 'Why didn't you ring yourself?'

'Because, my darling girl, you would have asked me things I didn't want to answer. Like where was I, what was I doing? And, rather than lie, I thought, like a fool, it would save an awful lot of hassle if I got David to do it. David, not realising how important it was, and having been unable to get through the first time he tried, asked Fabienne to do it.'

'Which, of course, she didn't.'

'No. And then that stupid tile slipped, and, instead of leaving me to come round normally, Jean-Marc carted me off to hospital!' he exclaimed in remembered disgust. 'As soon as I was able I discharged myself, went back to the house—and discovered that you'd been and gone! Lord, Melly, how can things get in such a muddle when you're trying to do things right?'

'I don't know,' she commented with a fond little smile.

'No, neither do I!'

'Go on,' she prompted gently.

'Right.' Turning to grin at her, he gave a little chuckle. 'I'm making a real meal of this, aren't I? Anyway, I drove to the airport, hung about for ages until the plane was ready, impatient and irritable, the mother and father of all headaches—and when I landed in England, hired a car to drive to

Beckford, I turned the radio on, and there was the news about the rail crash. I felt—oh, Melly, I don't think I can tell you how I felt. I was so sure, you see, that you would have been on it. When the announcer went on about how many had died I knew. I *knew*, Melly, that both you and Lauren were dead.'

'Oh, Charles!' she exclaimed softly. Sliding her arms round him, she held him tight.

'Punishment, that's what it was, I thought. My punishment for the way I'd behaved.' With a little shudder he returned her embrace; held her impossibly tight. 'And I hadn't told you! That was what I kept thinking, that I had never told you how I felt. That now you would never know!'

'And still don't,' she whispered. Easing herself away slightly, she looked up into his face.

'Don't?' he asked. 'Don't know that I love you? That you and Lauren are the most important things in my life? That without you, either of you, life wouldn't be worth living? When I walked into your mother's house, heard your voice, heard you defend me, I couldn't stop shaking. When I walked into the lounge, saw you sitting there, so white and tired and little, Lauren cradled on your lap, I wanted to cry. I haven't cried since I was a child, but I wanted to then.'

Standing very, very still in the circle of his arms, hardly daring to breathe, she stared at him in shock. Loved her? Charles loved her? Without her awareness, tears began to run slowly down her face.

'Ah, no,' he murmured thickly. 'Don't cry; please, don't cry.'

CHAPTER TEN

BENDING his head, Charles gently licked away the tears, and when Melly gave a little sob he quickly found her mouth with his. Hesitant at first, almost as if afraid of a rebuff, he slowly deepened the kiss; slowly released his pent-up breath.

Her heart hammering unevenly, her own breath stuck somewhere in her throat, she wound her arms round his neck, leaned against him, melted. She had thought she'd known, in dreams, in imagination, what it would feel like to be held like this, kissed like this—and she'd been wrong. Imagination could never convey the feeling of souls being fused, of bodies joining, of a man's special warmth, feel, taste, touch. Imagination could never convey the reality of drowning, submerging, or the subtle change to hunger, demand, until they both shook with the intensity of it.

Breaking the kiss, still holding her in the circle of his arms, he looked down into her dazed eyes. 'I have wanted to do that for a very long time,' he said shakily.

'So have I. I don't think you will ever know how much.'

'And still do, Melly?' he asked quietly. 'Still love?'

'Oh, yes. A different sort of love, perhaps, stronger, deeper. A love born of knowing you, understanding you. And it seems so impossible to believe that it's returned.'

'Not impossible. And why on earth shouldn't you believe? I've loved you for a very long time. Or, at least, it seems that way.'

'And is that really what you were going to tell me the night Nita came?'

'Yes. And to ask if there was any possibility of your loving me,' he added with a crooked grin. 'I didn't only want to leave the dinner party early that night because I thought you were tired, but because I wanted to tell you how I felt. Ask how you felt. I had it all worked out, how I was going to tell you that you were my anchor, my reason for being. That I liked coming home to you; liked the feeling of warmth you gave me; the feeling of need. I was going to extol my own virtues...' Resting his forehead against hers, he murmured, 'You're the one thing in my erratic life that is constant, never changing. My Melly. My friend. When I come home late, to know you're awake, listening for me... I can't tell you what a nice feeling it gives me...'

'How do you know I lie awake?' she whispered dazedly.

Leaning back, he gave another faint smile. 'I would quietly close the front door, quietly climb the stairs, and then I would wait, listening. I would hear you sigh, and then turn over in bed. The first time I thought perhaps I had woken you, so after that I would be extra careful not to make a noise; but still you would give that little sigh, and then turn over as though you were snuggling down under the covers. I used to imagine you smiling, giving a little nod of satisfaction that I was safely home... Foolish, hm?'

'No,' she breathed, 'because it was true.'

With another endearing smile he said, 'Thank you. The house doesn't feel the same without you in it. It feels an empty, cold place. There were so many years without my caring, Melly, without anything mattering very much—and then to find it and nearly lose it through my own stupidity. I have been so very afraid that it would be taken away.' His voice roughening, he added, 'I do love you, Melly. Here.' Taking her hand, he placed it over his heart. 'Here, inside of me; and here, in my mind.' Lifting her hand, he held it against his temple, then drew it down to press a kiss into the palm. 'I want to hold you, and love you; talk with you; be foolish. I want, when people are being outrageous, egotistic, to be able to glance at you, see the smile in your eyes, know you feel what I feel. I want to be—safe.' His voice thick, he tightened his hold.

Shivering with awareness of his masculine form pressed to her, she parted her mouth against his neck, touched her tongue to the warm flesh, and heard him groan deep in his throat.

Ducking his head, he urged her mouth upwards until he could claim it with his; could kiss her with urgency, desire, desperation almost, his arms an ever-tightening band around her.

Afraid to believe, afraid to let go, she poured all the long years of love into that embrace, gave back kiss for feverish kiss, until, breathing raggedly, they broke apart when the insistent knocking on the door finally registered. As they stared at each other Charles eventually gave a long, slow, shaky smile. 'Worth waiting for,' he said huskily.

Incapable of speech, aware only of the thud of her heart, the raggedness of her breathing, Melly just gazed up at him, and then smiled, in echo of his. Smiled as she had always wanted to smile at him. With love. 'Oh, Charles.'

When the knock came again louder, more insistent, they both jumped.

Still staring at her, he cleared his throat before calling, 'Come in.'

'*Merci*,' Jean-Marc approved with unusual sarcasm as he came into the room, carrying the baby. He looked decidedly fraught. With rather comic haste, he hurried across the room and handed the baby to her. 'She will not stop screaming! And she is very wet.'

Still feeling rather dazed, she apologised weakly, then thanked him. Glancing down at the now quiet, although red-faced baby, she carried her into the nursery to feed and change her. As she sat in the rocking-chair, her eyes on the mobiles hanging above the cot, another slow smile curved her mouth. He loved her. And later, when she had put Lauren down for the night, would he stay? A warm, delicious feeling of anticipation curling her insides, she shivered. Would he make love to her? Would he do all the things she had yearned for him to do? Would she now have the courage to touch him, love him, tell him all the things she had long wanted to say? Press her mouth to that strong throat...? With another long shiver, she tried to concentrate on the baby's needs. Looking down at the growing bundle in her arms, she smoothed her hand over the downy hair, traced a finger down the soft cheek, and remembered his words about his upbringing. So much she had to make up for.

She could hear the faint murmur of the men's voices from the bedroom, and as she finished feeding the baby and began to change her she suddenly felt shy of facing them both. Pressing the last studs closed on the sleeping suit, she picked Lauren up, gave her a final cuddle, and carried her back to the bedroom.

Charles was lying back on the bed, ankles crossed, hands linked behind his head, in an attitude of relaxation as he spoke to Jean-Marc, who was standing beside him. At her entrance Jean-Marc turned and smiled.

'All right?' he asked quietly, and when she nodded he wished her a quiet good night and left.

Glancing at Charles as he got to his feet and came to take the baby, she asked, 'Is everything all right? Or has Jean-Marc now decided he no longer likes babies?'

'No,' he laughed as he tucked Lauren warmly into the cot. 'He asked if he might stay.'

'He asked?'

'Mm hm.' Taking her hand, he led her to the bed and sat her on the edge. With his quirky smile he added, 'He seemed to have got the very odd idea that we might not want him any more.'

'Good heavens, why? Because of the baby?'

'No, because he has, of course, noticed, that we are—loving,' he said with a mischievous grin, 'and thought we might want to be on our own. I told him that we would be delighted for him to stay. He said he was greatly obliged, because he felt he was getting too old to be racketing around, and because he does not find me too overbearing—his words, not mine—and because he likes you very much, and he adores the baby. Well, he adores the baby when she is being good,' he re-phrased wryly. 'So, he would like to stay. Yes?'

'Of course. I can't imagine now how we could cope without him.'

'Good, then that's settled. Now, to more important things.'

'Like?' she asked with a rather wicked twinkle of her own.

Without answering, he put one arm round her back, one under her knees, and lifted her to lie full-length on the bed. Joining her, he said softly, 'Like making love to my wife.'

Touching her fingers gently to his face, then to his mouth, she murmured, 'I can't believe, after all the misunderstandings, the drama, that everything is now so perfect. I got so tired sometimes of trying to be all the things I thought you wanted me to be...'

'All I ever wanted was for you to be yourself,' he said gently.

'Yes, but *I* didn't know that. And now, after all this time, I begin to wonder if I know who myself is.'

'Well, *I* know,' he said firmly, 'and have no intention of waiting any longer while you try to puzzle it out, because, with my luck, the house will fall down, or the baby will wake up, or...'

Putting her hand across his mouth, her eyes laughing at him, she said softly, 'Stop wasting time.'

Removing her hand, he bit gently into the little finger. 'Stop being bossy. I'm in charge of this bit. Ready?'

'Yes.'

'Now?'

'Now.'

'Right.'

Next Month's Romances

Each month you can choose from a world of variety in romance with Mills & Boon. Below are the new titles to look out for next month, why not ask either Mills & Boon Reader Service or your Newsagent to reserve you a copy of the titles you want to buy — just tick the titles you would like to order and either post to Reader Service or take it to any Newsagent and ask them to order your books.

Please save me the following titles:	Please tick	√
A HONEYED SEDUCTION	**Diana Hamilton**	
PASSIONATE POSSESSION	**Penny Jordan**	
MOTHER OF THE BRIDE	**Carole Mortimer**	
DARK ILLUSION	**Patricia Wilson**	
FATE OF HAPPINESS	**Emma Richmond**	
THE ALPHA MAN	**Kay Thorpe**	
HUNGARIAN RHAPSODY (This book is free with THE ALPHA MAN)	**Jessica Steele**	
NOTHING LESS THAN LOVE	**Vanessa Grant**	
LOVE'S VENDETTA	**Stephanie Howard**	
CALL UP THE WIND	**Anne McAllister**	
TOUCH OF FIRE	**Joanna Neil**	
TOMORROW'S HARVEST	**Alison York**	
THE STOLEN HEART	**Amanda Browning**	
NO MISTAKING LOVE	**Jessica Hart**	
THE BEGINNING OF THE AFFAIR	**Marjorie Lewty**	
CAUSE FOR LOVE	**Kerry Allyne**	
RAPTURE IN THE SANDS	**Sandra Marton**	

If you would like to order these books from Mills & Boon Reader Service please send £1.70 per title to: Mills & Boon Reader Service, P.O. Box 236, Croydon, Surrey, CR9 3RU and quote your Subscriber No:..(If applicable) and complete the name and address details below. Alternatively, these books are available from many local Newsagents including W.H.Smith, J.Menzies, Martins and other paperback stockists from 11th September 1992.

Name:...

Address:..

....Post Code:.......................

To Retailer: If you would like to stock M&B books please contact your regular book/magazine wholesaler for details.

You may be mailed with offers from other reputable companies as a result of this application. If you would rather not take advantage of these opportunities please tick box ☐